Published by Discovery Association Publishing House
Chicago, Illinois

DAPH
P.O. Box 87662
Chicago, Illinois 60680

Library of Congress Control Number
2003108415

Ward 41: Tales of a County Intern
by John Raffensperger, M.D.

Summary: A pediatric surgeon fictionalizes dramatic and
sometimes disturbing experiences of his internship and
residency at the 1950s-era Cook County Hospital in Chicago.

ISBN: 1-931967-04-0

Manufactured in the United States of America
Printed by CSS Publishing Company, Lima, OH

Publisher's acknowledgements:
Editor: Joanne Sandelski
Cover Design: Steve McPheters

The names of all characters and specifics of circumstances
in these stories have been changed to
preserve patient confidentiality.

WARD 41:
TALES OF A COUNTY INTERN
BY JOHN RAFFENSPERGER, M.D.

WITH FOREWORD BY
DR. CORY M. FRANKLIN

TABLE OF CONTENTS

FOREWORD

In the decade after World War II, long before the television show *ER* brought medicine into the living room and made familiar heroes of doctors, highly motivated young medical students from all over the country migrated to large public hospitals built for the poor in order to learn and practice the craft of surgery. Practicing surgical and resuscitation techniques developed during the War, these students paved the way for today's medical heroes as they became their generation's top surgeons and mentors of today's leading surgeons. In *Ward 41: Tales of a County Intern*, John Raffensperger recounts the story of some of those young men at one of the country's legendary institutions, Cook County Hospital.

The stories in this book have the immediacy of a modern-day operating room while transporting the reader back to a different era. Dr. Raffensperger describes cases the modern resident is unlikely to encounter—patients dying after illegal abortions or from the effects of rheumatic fever. Time and again, the indigent are shunted away from other hospitals and forced to endure long waits just to be seen by a doctor. It was a time when routine antibiotics were too expensive for the poor (known as "charity patients," a term virtually unknown today, perhaps because charity has become a neglected virtue in the health care industry). There are characters from what sounds like a distant past—unwed mothers (another forgotten term), a Polish Cavalry General, an Old World syndicate henchman, a North Woods fisherman carrying the secret of buried treasure. In truth, it was not so long ago.

Even as Dr. Raffensperger describes the thrill of "the high" that young surgeons got operating on new trauma cases brought in all evening, he doesn't conceal the fact that working at Cook County Hospital in the 1950s was a struggle. The pay was bad and the working conditions, outdated equipment, and outmoded facilities were worse. Doctors transported their own patients through corridors several city blocks long. They bought their patients food and lent them money. There was deep gratitude but at the same time an element of danger was always lurking—one could die at the hands of a deranged patient or simply by contracting their disease. Despite all these travails, Dr. Raffensperger's stories are an elegy to an era and an environment that are gone forever. *Ward 41: Tales of a County Intern* is an embodiment of Oscar Wilde's adage, "What seem to us bitter trials are often blessings in disguise."

Cory M. Franklin, M.D.
Cook County Hospital

INTRODUCTION

Every patient has a story. Some are true. A doctor intervenes in the patient's story usually at a critical moment and for a very limited time. Often, especially for a young doctor, the patient's story becomes a part of the doctor's story and may have considerable influence upon his professional life.

These stories are based upon my experiences as a medical student, intern, naval medical officer, and surgical resident during the 1950s. Most of them involve patients for whom I cared at the Cook County Hospital. Until the advent of Medicare and the civil rights movement, few Chicago hospitals accepted charity patients, and the County was almost the only refuge for sick African Americans. The old Cook County Hospital, known affectionately as "The Old Lady on Harrison Street," was initially built to keep the "sick, poor, and other verminous people off the streets and away from the eyes of good citizens."

The inability of a poor mother to pay for her child's care is the basis for the rather naïve "Summer Romance." The romance is fictional, but I did once ply a nurse named Bonnie with martinis and have plunged scalpels into neck abscesses and then had nightmares about cutting the facial nerve.

My first patient as a medical student, seen after years of study, is the basis for "Romantic Heart." Rheumatic fever was common, especially among the poor in the days before streptococcal infections were routinely treated with penicillin.

"A Dissolute Life" describes an episode during ward rounds with an elderly surgeon in which he recounts the story of a colleague who contracted syphilis from a patient. Long before HIV became an issue, communicable diseases endangered medical personnel. Several medical students during my time contracted tuberculosis. I remembered the story of Dr. Herndon shortly after I had a needle-stick injury while operating upon a child with HIV.

A rotating internship exposes a young doctor to a wide variety of patients and diseases as well as his own shortcomings and frailties. I made many mistakes, but tried to learn from each patient, such as the old Polish general. The County was well known as a "teaching hospital," which meant that each patient was a teaching case. Patients paid for their care not in coin, but by allowing us to learn from their misfortunes. Sadly, sometimes, as in "A Teaching Case," the poor patient paid for his medical care with his life.

The young woman described in "Ward 41" reminds us of the terrible problems associated with the back-alley abortions in the days before Roe vs. Wade. Wealthy women had access to safe abortions, but the poor often died or became horribly ill at the hands of untrained practitioners. They could find help only at the Cook County Hospital.

"A Long Wait" is a true story, for which I continue to feel great shame, even though my behavior reflected a chronic lack of sleep.

Although I was not involved, a disgruntled patient did stab an intern to death. "A Cold Chinaman" also illustrates the problem of communicating with non-English speaking patients. Until recently, patients were simply told they needed an operation with very little discussion. There must have been many perplexed patients who awakened from an anesthetic without any idea of what had happened to them.

You may wonder why "Ship's Cat" is in this collection. I spent two years as a medical officer on an aircraft carrier after completing my internship. I had never personally performed an appendectomy, yet with the brash overconfidence of a Cook County intern, I felt that I could tackle any medical or surgical problem presented by man or beast and carried out several successful appendectomies on a tossing ship at sea. Now, fifty years later, I wonder whatever made me think that I could pull off major surgery in mid-ocean.

I returned to the Cook County Hospital in July 1956 to work as a surgical resident for four glorious years. During our fourth year, if we hadn't made too many mistakes, we residents became the exalted "night surgeons," which meant that we took care of all patients who required emergency surgery who came to the hospital at night. We reveled in operating upon people with gunshot wounds, appendicitis, perforated ulcers, or whatever weird problem came along. We worked until we were ready to drop, then drank coffee and started another day in the operating room. There was no surgical experience in the world quite like that at County.

The patients in these stories and their hospital surroundings were real. The wards were always crowded and dirty, there were never enough nurses or equipment, we residents were tired and busy, but the experience at "The Old Lady on Harrison Street" was great.

The boy described in "A Happy Ending" was one of those patients who made a career in surgery worthwhile, exciting, and challenging. The nurse and social worker in that story are just two of the wonderful people who made that old hospital work.

After a long dormant period, Jerry Cleaver of the Writer's Loft stimulated me to take up writing on a daily basis. I thank him for his excellent ideas, good teaching, and encouragement. Joanne Sandelski, my editor at DAPH, is really responsible for bringing this collection of stories out of the bottom drawer. She edited and organized them into their present form. I think she did a good job; Thanks, Joanne.

WARD 41:
TALES OF A COUNTY INTERN

ROMANTIC HEART

I had been through college plus a year and a half of medical school and still had not seen a patient, unless you count the cadaver that I had dissected with intimate familiarity during freshman anatomy. The class in physical diagnosis, or P-Dog, as it was called then, commenced in the middle of our sophomore year at medical school.

The first session covered taking a medical history and examination of the chest, heart, and lungs. My group of eight students was to meet our instructor in the intern's laboratory on Ward 65 at the County Hospital. Before class, we read six chapters in "Physical Diagnosis" by Cabot and Adams, an 888-page textbook. I read about taking a history and examination of the chest with minimal comprehension. There was a whole new vocabulary to learn in a very short time.

My roommates and I practiced auscultation and percussion of the chest on each other until we were more or less familiar with the normal heart and lungs. The upperclassmen shook their heads in sympathy when asked about Dr. Remenchek, the instructor. They said he had just finished his residency at the Presbyterian Hospital and was tough on students. Teaching sophomore students P-Dog was the first rung up the academic ladder to professor at the medical school.

For the first time we carried our black bags, gifts from the Eli Lilly drug company, with shining new stethoscopes, reflex hammers, blood pressure cuffs, a combination otoscope-ophthalmoscope, and a tuning fork to test for deep sensation. Ward 65 was in the men's medical building on an alley behind the main County Hospital. It had all the charm of a decayed tenement house. Two of us waited for the elevator while a nurse's aide tried to wheel in a stretcher carrying a comatose old man. The fat elevator operator worked a crossword puzzle and made no effort to help with the stretcher. All of the elevator operators were patronage workers—friends or relatives of the politicians. He took up a good bit of room in the small elevator. We finally crowded in and asked for Ward 65. We didn't talk or joke as we normally would going up to a class, as this was the real thing.

In the corridor on the ward, frazzled interns rushed about carrying syringes and test tubes. A red-haired nurse pushed a cart filled with medications toward the open ward. The intern's lab was a small room just off the corridor with tile floors and peeling green paint on the walls. Papers and hospital charts appeared to have been randomly flung at a desk along one wall. A centrifuge, racks of test tubes, and an open beaker of urine were on the lab bench next to the sink. The counter top was liberally splattered with old bloodstains and reagents.

A couple of our classmates were already seated on straight-backed metal chairs lined up in front of a faded blackboard. We piled our coats on an extra chair, sat down and tried to read the textbook. The rest of the students drifted in. All of us, even the guy who had been an army medic, were nervous and a little scared.

The instructor was late. He bustled into the room at eight-fifteen and took off his heavy overcoat. Dr. Remenchek, a young man, was short and a little stout with a high, intelligent forehead, black hair, and sallow skin. His dark suit was shabby, and a stethoscope peeked out from his coat pocket. He looked around the room and counted heads.

"Good! Everyone is here. We can start," he said.

He wrote "history" at the top of the blackboard with an exclamation point, underlined twice.

"Every patient encounter commences with the medical history. Most diagnoses are made with the history alone and the most important thing about the history is to establish rapport with the patient," he said.

He printed the word "RAPPORT" on the board in large block letters and hit the first letter with his chalk. He talked very rapidly and emphasized his points by writing a word or two on the board.

"First and most important, establish rapport, get to know your patient, put him at ease, then go into his chief complaint and the history of his present illness. Let the patient talk. It is important to put down in your history the patient's own words. Don't ask leading questions."

He was intense and went on to describe the review of systems, which amounted to asking about every possible symptom related to each organ system: dizziness, headaches, history of unconsciousness for the nervous system, and nausea, appetite, vomiting, pain, constipation, diarrhea, blood in the stool for the gastrointestinal tract.

Then, there was the family history. Every disease in each relative including grandparents and cousins had to be in our history. We were to inquire about the most personal aspects of the patient's life: how much he drank, sex, smoking, looking for anything that would shed light on his medical problems. He spoke rapidly, and I took notes as fast as possible, trying not to miss anything.

"Don't ever, ever write your history in front of the patient. It can make people nervous. Any questions?"

He looked around the class. One student raised his hand.

"Yes."

"Doctor, what are the best techniques to establish rapport?"

"Be polite, introduce yourself, ask about the patient's family, where he lives, his hobbies, pets, work, anything—just get him to talking. You have to get to know the patient," Dr. Remenchek said.

We all twisted on our chairs. Establishing rapport didn't seem like such a big deal.

"OK, now, I need a volunteer to demonstrate examining the heart and lungs."

There were no women in our group; in fact, there were only five in the class of one hundred fifty students. Years later, at Northwestern University, when an instructor called for a volunteer to demonstrate the topographic anatomy of the chest, a liberated, braless woman student slid her T-shirt over her head and was the first to volunteer. Our group had no such luck. There were no volunteers.

"You." Dr. Remenchek pointed to Bill Snyder.

Bill stood up and took off his tie, shirt, and undershirt. He had a nearly hairless chest, and his skin was pale as a coal miner. Medical students never spent Christmas vacation in Florida.

"First, inspect! Look at the shape of the chest, sternal retractions, unusual bulges, and watch how the patient breathes."

He demonstrated palpation for the apical impulse of the heart and how to outline the heart by percussion. He put one finger flat on the chest between two ribs and hit it with the middle finger of his other hand with a short, quick stroke. There was a hollow "plunk" when he percussed over the lung and a duller note over the heart. We learned where to best hear the opening and closing of the heart valves. The normal heart sounded like "lub-dup, lub-dup," and air coursing through the lungs made a nice rustling sound like a gentle wind in the leaves of an oak tree.

"OK, that wraps up this part of the session. Here are your patients."

He read off our names and our patients and their bed numbers from a notebook. I had Rufus Jones in bed 21.

"Remember, the important thing is to establish rapport, take a complete history, and examine the heart and lungs."

He checked his watch.

"At eleven, I will review your histories and go over your patients with you," he said.

We stood in a cluster in the corridor, lost and wondering where to go and how to start. There were large open rooms filled with patients at each end of the corridor. I asked a nurse's aide where to find Rufus Jones. She shook her head and didn't answer. Next, I tried an intern. He pointed to a large room at the north end of the corridor.

"The down ward, near the end," he said.

The huge ward smelled of unwashed bodies, stale urine, and overflowing bedpans. Beds stood along each wall and a double row ran down the middle of the ward. There was just space between beds for a small table and a chair. Despite frost on the windows, the wheezing radiators kept the room warm.

The patients, mostly old men, lay on their backs staring at the ceiling. Others sat on the bedside chairs. They smoked, hacked and spit dirty phlegm into open bottles. It was a dismal place. There wasn't a picture, radio, or book to cheer a sick man.

The patient in bed number one had an enormous barrel chest. He sat bolt upright with a rubber mask clamped on his face. The mask was connected by a rubber tube to a green oxygen canister. A hopeless, terrified look was in his eyes as he used every ounce of his strength to suck oxygen into his failing lungs. I walked down the narrow aisle, counting bed numbers.

"Hey Doc, kin ya spare a cig?"

The old man, one of the few standing beside his bed, had a bushy, yellow-stained beard. His hospital gown, which normally tied in the back, was on backward and was open, exposing faded blue, green, yellow and red tattooed dragons and snakes swirling around his chest. He held out his hand for the cigarette. A surprising, merry twinkle shone in his blue eyes.

"Sorry, I don't smoke," I said.

"Bet you can't guess what's wrong with me," he said.

He looked pretty healthy.

"No, I can't guess your diagnosis."

"I got sifeelus of the brain, caught it in China."

He went into a gale of laughter and slapped his leg. No one paid any attention, and I went on down the ward. The man in the next bed was sprawled on top of a blanket. His skin was a deep yellow, and his open pants disclosed an enormously distended abdomen. He probably had cirrhosis of the liver. Bed 21 was in a far corner of the ward next to a wall.

His name, Rufus Jones, was handwritten on the card attached to the end of his bed. He was young, a teenager, out of place among these old men. I wondered why he was not in pediatrics. Later, I learned that no matter what the patient's age or size, if he had pubic hair, he went to an adult ward. His skull and the bones of his face were fine and stood out under his skin. His eyes were deeply sunken and both arms were slender like two matchsticks.

Rufus sat bolt upright in his bed, his legs extended straight out under a gray blanket. His feet almost touched the rail at the end of the bed. His hands, with his clenched long bony fingers, rested on top of the blanket. The skin on his face and arms was smooth as if it had been rubbed with oil and was as dark as ebony. A rubber catheter taped to his nose led to a cylinder of oxygen at his bedside. I approached his bed and smiled.

"Mr. Jones, I'm Tom Slocum. I'm going to examine your chest. Have you been here long?"

He stared across the room and didn't answer. I tried again.

"It sure is cold today. You are lucky to be inside on a day like this."

His eyes moved toward me for an instant, but he said nothing.

"Ah, do you go to school?"

There was still no answer. I wasn't having much luck establishing rapport and commenced to realize there could be a problem. Perhaps he would talk about his illness.

"Mr. Jones, what brought you to the hospital?"

His lips didn't move but his mouth was open, and he made an audible sigh with each inspiration. I began to realize that he was very ill and that there was a wide cultural gap between this boy and me, a middle-class white man from a small town where there were no colored people. My excitement about seeing a live patient vanished. I tried again.

"What is wrong with you?"

He took several deep, sighing, rattling breaths and had a paroxysm of coughing. Spittle streaked with blood trickled down his chin.

"Ah---got---romantic--heart," he whispered.

Each word was spaced between several laborious noisy respirations.

I could barely make out his words and thought he was making some kind of a joke. He wouldn't say anything more. In desperation, I peeked at the chart on a clipboard at the foot of his bed. Taking information from the chart was strictly forbidden. The intern's note was a hasty scrawl on a couple of pages.

"This is a known case of rheumatic heart disease, admitted because of shortness of breath and swollen legs."

A few more sentences described rales in his lungs and a variety of heart murmurs. On the last page was the diagnosis. "Rheumatic heart disease, in failure." For treatment, the intern had ordered bed rest, digitalis, morphine, and mercury diuretics.

I had read about rheumatic fever and had studied a mitral valve under the microscope in pathology. The edge of the valve was curled and covered with scar tissue. Rheumatic fever was some sort of reaction that followed a bout of streptococcal tonsillitis or scarlet fever. It could affect the brain or joints, but mainly it damaged the mitral and aortic valves as well as the ventricular muscle of the heart. The mitral valve became scarred and narrow, closing off the flow of blood from the left atrium into the ventricle. The aortic valves were stiff and retracted so that blood regurgitated backwards from the aorta into the heart.

"Is it OK if I check your pulse and examine your chest?" I asked.

He barely nodded his head. His hand was ice cold and I had a hard time finding his radial artery. I had learned to count the pulse in first aid classes, but I had never felt anything like this. I lost count at one hundred twenty and it was very irregular; bump-bump-bump---------bump-bump----bump--bump---bump----------bump. Most beats were almost too weak to count, but some were hard and strong. A couple of times, there was such a long interval between beats that I thought he was dead. I lifted his lifeless hand from the bed and felt for the pulse with the fingers of my other hand. There was a slight tightening of his fingers around my hand. His dark eyes fluttered, then looked into mine.

"OK, now I am going to check your heart and lungs," I said.

There was no response and I came to realize he was near to death. Perhaps he realized this. I untied the gown at the back of his neck and let it fall to his waist.

Each rib stood out, as prominent as the timbers of a half-completed ship, and his heart pounded against the rib cage. The apex beat was at the left lateral edge of his chest. I placed the middle finger of my left hand on his chest and tapped it with my right index finger, just as the instructor had demonstrated. The note was a dull thump, not the hollow sound that he had elicited. I tried again, thinking that I was doing it wrong. The tone was still a dull "thump."

I took the new, neatly folded stethoscope out of my black bag and inserted the earpieces. They were uncomfortable, but I gingerly placed the bell over his right lung. The sound was like water gurgling through pipes, with an occasional finer sound as if pieces of cloth were being rubbed together. It was totally mystifying and sounded nothing like my classmate's chest.

The heart sounds were even stranger. There was a continuous rumble over his entire heart. I couldn't make out systole or diastole. There was an especially loud noise over the aortic area. I had to lean over his body to listen and when I stood up, the blanket came away from his legs. They were grotesquely swollen up to his knees. I replaced the blanket and retied the gown with a bowknot. It was time to go back to the lab and write up my findings. There wasn't much to say.

"Thanks. Don't worry, you will be OK," I said.

I hurried back to the intern's lab and sat down with the clipboard and blank sheets of paper. For the history, I simply wrote "romantic heart." There was nothing about his present illness, past history, or family history. My description of his heart and lungs wasn't much better. The other students were furiously writing page after page in their histories and physicals. I was certainly going to flunk the course.

Dr. Remenchek returned promptly at eleven o'clock and collected our papers. He quickly went through them, nodding, sometimes saying, "good, good." Once he exclaimed, "excellent work." He came to my history and frowned.

"What's this? Slocum, is this the best you could do?"

I explained how difficult it was for the boy to talk and how sick he was.

"Let's go see this patient and show you how to perform a proper history and physical examination," he said.

We gathered our new black bags and followed the instructor down the ward to Rufus Jones. Except for more of the blood stained spittle on his chin, he was exactly as I had left him.

"I am Dr. Remenchek with some visitors to see you."

Without saying a word, the Doctor pulled away the blanket and studied the boy's swollen feet. He shifted his gaze to his neck and then loosened his gown so he could see the chest. All eight of us were arrayed around the bed, but Rufus Jones seemed to take no notice of us. Perhaps he was accustomed to medical students and interns.

"Oh, this is a very good case—just beautiful, lovely clinical signs. Look at the distended neck veins, a sign of right heart failure, and note the strong pulsations of the carotid arteries, definitely a Corrigan's pulse—indicates aortic regurgitation," Dr. Remenchek said.

He stabbed the air with his finger, pointing at me.

"Slocum, look at his chest and tell us what you see."

I was at a total loss and didn't know what he wanted me to say. The other students shuffled their feet and looked at the bare chest with great intensity and were glad that they had not been asked the question.

"Sir, he is very slender and he is breathing very fast. Also, his heart is thumping pretty strong," I said.

"Is that all? That thumping is his cardiac apex, which is displaced all the way to his mid-axillary line, an indication of right ventricular hypertrophy."

Dr. Remenchek percussed Jones's chest and listened to his lungs and heart with his stethoscope, then had each student listen and describe what he heard. We spent the next forty-five minutes listening to the various rales in the lungs and to the systolic rumbling murmur over the mitral valve and the loud diastolic murmur at the aortic area. I still could not tell one murmur from another, but nodded as if I had heard everything he described. He then demonstrated the edema, which left a "pit" after he had pressed the skin over Jones's ankle with one finger. He counted the pulse for a full minute and smiled.

"Well, Slocum, you surely counted the pulse. What did you make out of it?"

"It was real fast and hard to count," I said.

"Take the pulse again. It has irregular-irregularity, diagnostic for atrial fibrillation, a bad sign."

During all of this, he did not say a word to Rufus Jones. He reviewed the physical findings once again.

"What we have here are all the classic signs of rheumatic heart disease in severe failure. He has mitral valve stenosis and aortic regurgitation with an enlarged left atrium and bi-ventricular hypertrophy. The rales we hear in the lungs are fluid, a combination of heart failure and pneumonia. Great case!"

Dr. Remenchek folded his stethoscope and walked away down the ward. The other students turned and followed. I stayed behind long enough to retie Rufus's gown behind his neck. His eyes seemed to be focused on some distant point across the ward, and his breathing was even more ragged and difficult. I caught up with Dr. Remenchek in the lab as he was putting on his coat.

"Is there anything else to do for him?" I asked.

He seemed almost angry at the question, as if therapy was not a part of the day's curriculum.

"Not one damn thing," he said.

I arrived early for the next class on Ward 65, which was on the physical examination of the head and neck. Another patient was in bed 21. One of the interns said the boy had died and that the autopsy had shown severe heart disease and pneumonia. Dr. Remenchek was a good diagnostician, but I did not think much of his ability to establish rapport.

I thought about skipping class that afternoon and getting drunk at the Greek's. I had a dollar and a half in my pocket and double martinis were only seventy-five cents. Instead, I went to our usual Wednesday pathology laboratory and then to the library. It was a relief to study bits and pieces of human beings under the microscope and much easier to read about disease in the textbooks than to see it in real life.

SUMMER ROMANCE

The young woman sat on a hard wooden bench in the corridor outside the emergency room, rocking a crying child on her lap. It was a late Saturday afternoon, the day's work was over and she was the only patient in the waiting area. Dr. Weaver and the nursing supervisor walked ahead, chatting and laughing. I paused, curious. The woman put out her hand, palm upwards.

"Won't you please help?"

"What's wrong?" I asked.

"My baby is very sick and they won't look at her. They said that I have to go to the County Hospital."

"Who said that?"

She gestured at the stiff, starched back of the nursing supervisor retreating down the hall.

"I don't have any money and the nurse said they don't take charity cases here."

The mother's cheeks were puffy. With her free hand she wiped tears away from her eyes. The little girl had curly blond hair and was a year or so old. Her head was turned toward her mother, showing a red and swollen neck.

"What's wrong with her?" I asked.

"Last week a doctor said she had a sore throat and gave her some penicillin. Now her neck is swollen, she can't sleep, and the fever won't go down."

When I touched the hard swelling, the baby screamed. I had only heard about it in lectures, but it looked like an abscess which needed to be drained.

It was late afternoon, and I had spent all day helping Dr. Weaver, a general practitioner who did quite a lot of surgery. When we finished in the operating room, he took me to the emergency department to help remove a mole. It was only a small thing, but the patient said it was ugly and she couldn't wear her new off-the-shoulder dress. It absolutely had to come off. Dr. Weaver solicitously injected extra Novocain before snipping off the mole and he fussed over the skin sutures. She was terribly worried over the scar.

"Now, now, no one will notice the scar. You will be just lovely in the new dress," Dr. Weaver said.

He had oozed sympathy while applying a Band-Aid over the tiny incision.

Dr. Weaver and the ER nurse had turned the corner. I didn't know what to do, but it seemed wrong to send the baby all the way to the County Hospital, when she was right here.

"Your child has pus which needs to be drained, but all the attending surgeons have gone home," I said.

She shook her head and dabbed at her eyes with a wet handkerchief.

"I don't even know how to get to the County Hospital."

The child needed a small incision to drain the abscess. I had watched an intern at the County Hospital drain a large carbuncle, and thought that it couldn't be too much different. The student nurse in the treatment room was a big, pleasant red-faced country girl. I had joked with her a couple of times, so I told her about the child and told her to get Novocain and sterile instruments. She was already boiling the scalpel and forceps from the last patient.

"Who is the attending doctor?"

"There isn't one."

"Get the resident."

"He's still busy in the OR," I answered.

Although I was wearing a white surgical scrub suit complete with a cap and a mask, she knew that I was only a medical student. A half-dozen students worked at the hospital during the summer for experience and to earn money. We were not supposed to treat patients by ourselves.

The student nurse listened to the baby's screams and after a moment's hesitation shrugged her shoulders.

"Okay, I might get canned, but let's do it," she said.

The mother brought the screaming, kicking baby into the treatment room and put her on the treatment table.

"You want the child bundled?" the nurse asked.

I nodded. She expertly wrapped a sheet around the child's body, so that her arms were held down to her side and her legs were immobilized. She looked like a little mummy with only her head and neck exposed.

The nurse told the mother to leave the room. I swabbed the skin with iodine and covered the child's face and chest with towels. The freshly sterilized instruments were laid out on a sterile towel. The nurse held the child's head. I pulled on rubber gloves and injected Novocain into the skin over the swelling. The child looked around the room with large frightened eyes and her screams reached an impossible crescendo of frantic sound.

My incision barely scratched the skin. I bore down on the scalpel and blood flowed in two rivulets down the side of her neck. There was still no pus. Sweat rolled down my face and onto the mask. My glasses began to fog.

"Oh God, I really screwed up this time," I thought.

I cut deeper, then poked a blunt hemostat through the next layers. There was a gush of thick yellow pus and I realized that I had not taken a breath since the first tentative incision. The rest was easy. With a hemostat, I spread the wound and pushed in a rubber drain. The nurse handed me some sterile gauze pads and the two of us wrapped the child's neck with a heavy bandage.

The child went to sleep as soon as her mother picked her up. I told her to apply hot towels over the bandage three times a day and come back in two days to have the dressing changed. The young mother mumbled her thanks and left with the sleeping child over her shoulder.

Later, in the doctor's dining room, I bragged about my surgical triumph to a couple of fellow students. Chuck, the smartest and most thoughtful guy in our class, stabbed the air with a fork filled with mashed potatoes.

"Did you identify the facial nerve?"

"Ah, no, I guess not," I answered.

"I hope you didn't cut it," was his laconic reply.

My nightmares awake and asleep for the next two days was of a beautiful blond girl whose face was ugly and distorted by a severed facial nerve. I had visions of her drooping mouth, the flat expressionless face and an eye which she could not close. I hardly slept or ate. A part of the facial nerve runs through the upper neck, almost directly beneath my incision. I cursed myself for not sending her to the County Hospital, or at least, for not calling the resident.

I mechanically scrubbed up for the operating room, held retractors and cut sutures, all the time wondering if I would be kicked out of the hospital, or even out of medical school. Could medical students be sued? By operating on the child I was guilty of practicing without a license and probably faced a long jail term.

Two days later, when the same student nurse took the mother and her child into the treatment room, my little patient smiled. The facial nerve was perfectly alright. The inflammation was gone, and her fever was down. I was flooded with an incredible sense of joy and relief.

The little girl sat on her mother's lap while I changed the bandage. Until then I had not paid much attention to her mother. She was tall, perhaps nineteen or twenty years old, but was dressed like a high school student with a pleated blue skirt and a high-necked white blouse.

"I don't even know your name. We didn't make any records for the emergency room. I'm Tom Slocum," I said.

"I am Bonnie Dormaine, and this is Marie."

She leaned forward and gave me a dazzling smile. "We can't thank you enough. Marie is a different child."

Marie wiggled and gurgled and then clung to her

mother's shoulder, but she turned and stole another look at me before she again snuggled against her mother.

I felt very happy and laughed out loud for the first time in days.

"Keep up the hot soaks and come back at the same time in a couple of days."

When she returned, the baby was fine and the wound almost healed. Her mother wore shorts and sandals and a low-cut blouse. She had an absolutely gorgeous body, and when she leaned over to hold Marie, the top of her blouse opened. She had high cheekbones, lovely full lips, gray eyes and was quite beautiful. I must have blushed because she laughed at my consternation. There was only a high school ring on her finger. I wondered about her husband.

The wound required only a Band-Aid, but I thought wildly for some reason to see her again.

"Sometimes these abscesses come back. You should return on Saturday."

I watched her long slim legs as she walked down the hall and out of the emergency room and was overcome with adolescent lust.

In high school, I had been a gangly bookworm and the girls liked basketball players. College hadn't been much better. There had only been passionate necking in sorority house parlors under the watchful eyes of housemothers who were determined to preserve the girls' virginity. The first two years of medical school had been one neverending grind of dissecting cadavers, lectures, books and labs. It didn't take long to find

out that the graduate nurses were out for interns or residents
and that the student nurses had curfews and housemothers
which limited the opportunities. Now I had a job at Austin
General, a private hospital, as a sort of sub-intern. I had high
hopes for "making out." Unfortunately, the graduate nurses
were older women, and the students were affiliated with a
bible college. Their idea of a good time was a Wednesday night
prayer meeting.

I went to the emergency room early, but she didn't
come in at four. A half-hour later, an older woman with a
teenage girl holding Marie arrived. The woman said that Bonnie
had to work until six that night, and so she had brought the
baby in for her appointment. The wound was healed and the
child was perfectly normal. I could hardly conceal my
disappointment over not seeing Bonnie.

"Why didn't Mr. Dormaine come in with the baby?" I
asked.

"Bonnie isn't married," the woman said.

"Uh, where does she work?"

The teenage girl picked up the baby. They turned to
leave.

"Wieboldt's, in Oak Park," said the older woman.

I changed out of the scrub suit into my best slacks and
sport shirt and caught the Lake Street bus. Wieboldt's was a
big general department store at the corner of Lake and Harlem.
It was a huge box of a building and I wandered aimlessly on
the first floor until I spotted Bonnie in the women's clothing
section. It took a great deal of courage to walk up to her, as if

I was just passing through or on a shopping trip. I tried to act surprised at seeing her.

"Hi," I said.

She wore a dark blue skirt and high-necked blouse and her hair was drawn back in a severe pony tail. She was surprised. It was an awkward moment and she blushed.

"I'm sorry I couldn't bring Marie, but I had already taken a lot of time off."

"She looked just fine. The wound is healed."

Bonnie smiled and came out from behind the counter.

"Yes, she doesn't have a temperature and eats everything."

I felt like a fool and looked around the store, perhaps for a necktie or something to buy. Finally, I blurted it out.

"I don't have to work tonight. Could we have dinner?"

She put her hand over her mouth.

"Oh, no, I have to take care of Marie."

"Can't you get a babysitter?"

She had a sort of dreamy look and put a woman's blouse back on a hanger.

"It would be nice to go out. I can call and see if Betty will take care of her a little while longer."

While she finished working, I looked in the windows at Marshall Field's across the street and then walked through the park on River Forest side of Harlem. She finally came out of Wieboldt's by the Lake Street entrance.

We took a cab to the Black Angus, a steak house, just a few blocks south of the hospital. The waiter pulled out a table with a flourish and seated us side by side against the wall. There was a good Saturday night crowd with a lot of noise and laughter.

"How about a martini?" I asked.

"I never had one. Are they good?"

"Sure," I said, "especially if you like olives."

She brushed against my arm.

"I adore olives."

She made a face at the first sip, but after we finished the first drink, we had another with the steaks. We ate ravenously and talked nonstop. Mostly, I told her about the hospital and surgery. She laughed at silly jokes and said that she was from Valparaiso, Indiana, and had finished two years of nurse's training.

"How about another drink?"

She giggled.

"Sure."

About half way through the meal I reached over and kissed her behind the ear. She took my hand in both of hers and brought it to her lips. We sat very close and I was very aware of her warm soft body.

I paid the bill and tipped the waiter with my last dollar.

She stumbled on the way out the door.

"Whoops, too many martoonys."

We laughed and held each other. Bonnie lived on Waller Street in Chicago, a dozen blocks away. It felt like rain, and a rising wind agitated the trees which cast dark, restless shadows on the streets. We flung ourselves on a bench and kissed passionately. I caressed the bare skin of her back and she feverishly opened the buttons of my shirt. We rubbed against one another and she moaned until she suddenly pulled away.

"Oh my God, what time is it?"

It was almost midnight. She pushed me aside, got up and began walking rapidly down the dark street.

"I forgot about Marie."

As we turned in to her house, I grabbed her hand.

"Can I see you tomorrow? We can go out for a soda in the afternoon," I asked.

She hesitated.

"We can take Marie," I said.

"OK," she answered.

"Is two all right?"

She nodded.

I felt wonderful in the morning and rushed through rounds on Dr. Weaver's patients. None were very sick but they all whined and complained. I had to spend a lot of time listening to Mrs. Heplewhite complain about her breakfast and cold tea. She was a fat, rich woman, who had a backache and was always propped up on pillows and wearing a pink nightgown. Dr. Weaver often put women in the hospital for minor aches and pains for X-rays and tests. They had the most expensive private rooms and were a greater nuisance than the really sick patients. I called him at ten to go through the list of his patients. He asked questions about temperatures, pain, and incisions. I knew most of the answers.

"Did Mrs. Heplewhite move her bowels?"

"Um, well, I didn't ask."

"Young man, you must always ask about a patient's bowels. It makes them think you really care."

I took a long shower, borrowed my roommates after-shave lotion, and put on a clean white shirt and my best slacks.

Waller Street was a few blocks east of Austin Avenue, in an old neighborhood of once-fine homes. The sidewalk was uneven where tree roots had grown under the concrete. Bonnie's house was typical of the decayed neighborhood. It had been covered with artificial brick shingles. An outside staircase, tacked on as an afterthought, led to her second floor apartment.

She met me at the door, balancing Marie on one hip. She wore the shorts and low-cut blouse again and was perfectly lovely.

It was a long, hot walk to Peterson's ice cream parlor, and the baby cried. I carried her for a while and was amazed at how heavy she was. We ordered sundaes and cokes and talked of odds and ends. Marie entertained us by smearing ice cream on her face.

On the way home, we stopped in a small park so Marie could play in a sand box. Bonnie was thoughtful and a bit standoffish. I had hoped that she would invite me in, but she stopped on the sidewalk outside her house and thanked me for the ice cream.

"I work tomorrow night, but have Tuesday off. Would you like to see a movie?"

"I don't think so," she said.

"Well, how about Wednesday?"

She looked doubtful, but before she went up the stairs, she said.

"I'll see if I can get a baby sitter."

She did not get a baby sitter, but on Wednesday she invited me to her apartment. Her landlady lived on the first floor and had a couple of teenage daughters. Bonnie called her "Aunt Betty," and the girls baby sat for Marie when she worked. There was a parlor, with a kitchenette in the back and a bedroom. It was plainly furnished, a little untidy, and smelled of diapers and baby food. The window to the street was open and an electric fan brought a breath of coolness to the June evening.

She turned off the radio and put on a stack of popular songs and light operetta on the record player. She made iced tea and fed the baby, and then put her down in a crib in the bedroom. I leafed through a *Life* magazine and glanced at stories about the war in Korea until she brought the tea. She was warm and damp but wore a pale shade of lipstick and had on a bit of perfume. We talked idly about the hospital and demanding customers at her store. She let me take her hand until the baby cried. At the door, she turned her face and I kissed her cheek. We agreed to go out for dinner again on the weekend.

I thought of her incessantly, but was busy every day and worked every third night. One of Dr. Weaver's patients hemorrhaged after a hysterectomy and he had to call in a specialist to operate again. It was a terrible night and the woman almost died. I realized then that Dr. Weaver was not a very good surgeon even though he had a big practice and his patients adored him. It was a rude awakening to find that not all doctors were altruistic.

We medical students got our first check for a hundred dollars on the first of July. I felt as rich as a king and took Bonnie to an ornate Italian restaurant on Rush Street. We had martinis again, and chianti with chicken cacciatore and ravioli. She wore a new white short-sleeved cotton sweater and a tight skirt. Her perfumed hair was loose and brushed her shoulders. I snuggled closer.

"You are beautiful."

She touched an acne scar on her cheek.

"It's a good thing you didn't know me when I was younger."

After dinner, we held hands and walked down to the lake to look at the stars. Suddenly we were kissing passionately and clinging to one another. She had tears on her cheek.

"I am so happy," she said.

We kissed in the back seat of a taxi all the way to her house. She got the baby from Betty on the first floor and put her down in the crib with a bottle. She put on a record, "Kisses Sweeter than Wine," and turned out the light. We kissed and necked, but when I tried to go farther, she pushed me away and said I had to leave.

She was always in my dreams and daydreams. Thinking about her, I would forget to cut sutures until the surgeon said, "Wake up, dummy." I would have spent every available minute with her, but sometimes she held back and had an excuse for not going out or inviting me in. This only increased my passion.

One Sunday, we took Marie on the Lake Street elevated train and rumbled downtown, past the backs of abandoned factories and dumps filled with wrecked cars. The train screeched and jerked around the loop and we got off at Monroe Street, then walked over to Michigan Avenue and took a bus to the North Avenue beach. Bonnie looked great in a swimming suit. She didn't swim, but sat on the beach, playing in the sand with the baby. I waded into the ice-cold lake, shivered, but swam a little, then got out and dried in the sun. We bought cokes and hot dogs from a rickety pushcart. Noisy teenage boys ran and kicked sand.

The trip back on the elevated train was hot and sticky. The baby cried and needed a diaper change. We were all tired. Bonnie left me on the sidewalk, feeling very frustrated. We had some good times, like the night I took her to the Tip Top Tap in the Allerton Hotel. We sipped gin and tonics while watching the lights of buildings blinking in the night and the car lights moving steadily up Michigan Avenue. She was always reticent, but did say that "Aunt Betty" was a family friend from Valparaiso who helped her out after she "got into trouble."

She would neck passionately one night and be cold the next. She pushed me away when I tried to get into her underpants. I was frustrated as hell and couldn't understand what was wrong.

She listened to the news broadcasts and sometimes seemed to have been crying. President Truman announced progress toward a ceasefire, but the war went on.

I was hot for her and thought of marriage, but didn't know how to support a wife and child through two more years of medical school and an internship. The idea of explaining the situation to my starchly upright small-town parents was not pleasant.

Leaves began falling from the trees, and my roommate and I arranged to work every third night at Austin General while going to school. We were assigned to start the junior medicine clerkship at the Research Hospital the second week in September.

A few days later, we went out to a pizza joint in the early evening. While walking back to her place, I told her about the clerkship and starting school again. She stopped under a streetlight.

"Aren't you already a doctor?"

"Well, not exactly, I have two more years to go."

"Oh, I thought you were an intern."

She said no more and went up the stairs to her apartment, leaving me on the street.

I had to work the next night, but hurried over to Waller Street as soon as I could get away from the hospital. There was no answer when I knocked. Betty, the landlady called out from behind her screen door.

"Who's there?"

"It's me—Tom. Where's Bonnie?"

"Bonnie ain't here no more. She took a bus this morning to meet her boyfriend on a ship comin' into San Diego."

A DISSOLUTE LIFE

Dr. Ferguson told this story when I was a senior surgical clerk on Ward 54. It was his last year to make rounds at County. He died a year or so later. Dr. Ferguson was an old Rush professor, presumably in his late seventies at the time, because he had graduated from Rush Medical College during the late 1890s. After an internship at County, he studied with great surgeons such as John B. Murphy, then went to England to learn orthopedics.

Dr. Ferguson joined the British Army at the beginning of the First World War and later, in 1917, was in charge of a United States Army base hospital. He was tall, with distinguished white hair, but like many surgeons who had spent a lifetime over an operating table, he had a pronounced stoop. He was one of the true old-time general surgeons who did a bit of everything from bellies to bones and had a great Michigan Avenue practice.

Ward 54 was clean and well-run. Sometimes there was even a night nurse because Dr. Ferguson had buddies who were politicians. The Professor didn't do surgery any more, but watched the residents operate. After the cases were finished, he came to the ward to see patients with the housestaff and students. He was a great teacher, one who exposed us to the art and humanity of medicine because he took great personal interest in each patient. The old men with inoperable cancers always seemed to feel better after he had talked with them for a while.

I was there during the wintertime and the ward was filled with derelicts suffering with leg ulcers and frostbite. Some of the old-timers managed to get admitted to the ward each winter. He remembered them and they called him Dr. Sam. The residents showed him the problem patients, for whom he invariably came up with the right diagnosis.

His ability to solve clinical problems seemed almost like magic, but it was because of his long experience and the time he spent examining patients. But Dr. Ferguson had one very annoying habit. He insisted that the intern bring a cart with a basin of water, green soap, and a bottle of alcohol along on rounds. Between each patient, he washed, rinsed with alcohol and then dried his hands with a fresh towel. If the intern forgot the cart, he would walk the length of the ward to the only sink and wash his hands between every patient.

One afternoon, a student asked him why he went to so much trouble just to wash his hands. We were all standing around a bed. I have forgotten what was wrong with the patient, but it doesn't matter.

"I'll tell you why I wash my hands, and don't any of you ever forget it. I was there when it all began. Afterwards, I pieced together the tragic story of Professor Herndon. You probably never heard of him, but he is still quoted in some of the books.

It started in the amphitheater of the old County Hospital, the one built in 1876. The Rush doctors had bribed the County politicians to build the amphitheater, so we students could have a place to see patients with the professors.

I was in my last year as a student. We came tumbling down the steep amphitheater stairs, eager to get the best places close to the "pit." My classmates and I were still young and enthusiastic, and our pockets were stuffed with pencils and notebooks. The Thursday evening clinics were the highlight of the week: a chance to see real live patients rather than listening to everlasting lectures. The boys in the front rows were settling into their seats, joking and asking, 'what's the case?'

I was there early, anxious to be in the front row. More students rushed in, out of breath, jostling and pushing. Someone in the back row stole his neighbor's book and tossed it down the aisle.

The Rush professors put on a good show. Only a week before, Jonathan Kerr, the great surgeon, had fired a bullet into the skull of a cadaver to demonstrate the effects of gunshot wounds. Bits of bone flew into the amphitheater, much to our glee.

Two interns, only a little older than us students, wheeled in the cart with the first patient. Martin, the big red-haired farm boy next to me noisily shelled and ate peanuts. He threw the shells on the floor. I gave him a nudge in the ribs, and said, 'shut up.'

The patient, a young man in his early thirties, was on the cart, his lower body covered with a coarse blanket. His folded hands held a bible. He was slender, with a pale face and fair hair. He was not like the usual rough-cut County patient. The interns arranged the cart so that the patient lie facing the students under the bright gaslight.

We became instantly quiet and attentive as the professor strutted into the room. Dr. Richard Herndon was stocky, with black hair, dark eyes, and a handsome, ruddy, clean-shaven face. He wore a dark waistcoat and a fashionable fawn-colored vest from which hung a heavy, gold watch-chain. His brightly polished black shoes reflected the gaslights. He had graduated from Rush Medical School at the top of his class and had taken the first place in the examination for the Cook County Internship. Johann Metzger, the great diagnostician and surgeon, recognized Herndon's intelligence and hard work and took him under his wing.

Professor Herndon studied for a year and specialized in internal medicine instead of doing general practice or surgery like most of us in those days. He was a professor at Rush and lectured on diseases of the heart and lungs. Herndon was a great showman and gave dramatic lectures. He loved the County clinics, where he demonstrated his amazing skill as a diagnostician. The interns brought out their most difficult cases, hoping to trip him up. The millionaires on Prairie Avenue sought him out because he had a warm bedside manner, which appealed to the ladies.

He glanced at the patient, then fixed his eyes on the intern, a tall, gangly fellow.

'What is this man's history?' he asked.

It was more of a command than a request. The professor stood with his chin in his hands.

'Sir, the patient is thirty years old. He complains of a fever and a swelling in his neck. He doesn't want to eat and is very nervous. The lymph nodes in his neck are enlarged. The ward doctors think he may have bovine tuberculosis or some sort of tumor.'

Professor Herndon twirled his watch-fob.

'And why did you think of tuberculosis?'

The intern stammered and gestured with his clumsy hands.

'He is...he is...from a small town in...a...Wisconsin and lives near a herd of cows.'

The professor laughed as if the intern had made a great joke.

'What is this young man doing in Chicago?'

The poor flustered intern shuffled his feet and stared at a spot on the far wall.

'He is ah...ah stud-studying at Mac-MacCormick sem-seminary to become a Presbyterian minister.'

Some of the students chuckled and nudged their neighbor. Others laughed out loud. A student in the back row struck a match and lit a cigar, then blew smoke. We were an irreverent lot in those days.

Without another word, the professor pulled up the cuffs of his coat and felt the patient's neck with strong blunt fingers.

'Yes, the lymph nodes are enlarged and movable.'

He asked the patient, 'Does this hurt?'

The young man shook his head.

'No, no pain.'

Professor Herndon turned to the assembled students and flicked his watch-chain.

'The lymph nodes are non-tender.'

He then drew down the blanket and had the patient sit up, while he examined the chest and abdomen. He grunted and then looked into the patient's mouth.

He exclaimed, 'Aha, just as I suspected.'

With his right hand, he pulled down the patient's lower lip, and with his left index finger, minutely felt a sore, which was rather like an ulcer, just inside the patient's mouth.

He motioned to the intern.

'Palpate this.'

The intern moved to the cart and put his finger in the patient's mouth.

'Is the ulcer hard or soft?'

'Hard, sir.'

'Well, what is it then?'

'I ai-ain't, I am not sure, sir.'

The students snickered and some laughed out loud. We had great fun at the intern's expense, but within a few months we would be in the same boat. Again, Professor Herndon felt the lesion with his left index finger, the same one he had cut while slicing a lemon for his evening toddy the night before.

He motioned to the students in the front row.

'Gentlemen, come examine this patient. Please note the hard consistency of the ulcer and its elevated edges. It is completely painless.'

He waited while several of the students examined the patient and then made a flourish with his hands.

'Gentlemen, this is the classic primary chancre of syphilis.'

The students gasped and the patient listened in stunned disbelief, then burst out crying.

Over the next few weeks, the *Chicago Times* carried stories about the forthcoming marriage of Professor Herndon to Maude Baker, daughter of a prominent businessman.

It was a big story around the school. Everyone wondered when he had time to court the daughter of a rich man. We thought he was marrying her for the money, but she was a good-looking woman. Sometimes she came with him to the Presbyterian hospital when he made rounds on his patients.

One day, at the hospital, he complained about an ulcerated pimple on his finger. It didn't hurt and went away, so he didn't bother about it.

They were married in St. Patrick's and held the reception at the Baker mansion on Ashland Avenue. The gossip columns made a big thing out of it. The mayor and all of the Rush doctors were there, rubbing elbows with businessmen and politicians.

They sailed on a steamship to Europe for a long honeymoon combined with visits to the famous hospitals in Vienna and Heidelberg. During the Atlantic crossing, he complained to a friend that he was feverish and tired. He attributed these symptoms to a touch of 'mal de mer' and too much to drink.

In Vienna, they stayed at the Hotel Sacher where his

bride reveled in the heyday of Viennese music and culture. She happily visited museums and bought elegant dresses. He attended clinics at the Allgemeines Krankenhaus and visited with his old professors. In the afternoons, they strolled hand-in-hand through the old inner city. They kept an eye on the medieval spire of Stephansdom as a guide back to the hotel.

One afternoon, with heads together listening to a waltz, they saw Emperor Franz Joseph dash by in his golden carriage. Every evening there were concerts and balls, where visiting American physicians were welcomed as distinguished guests. They were a handsome and popular couple. Many years later, one of the Rush doctors who had been there at the same time told me that part of the story.

Near the end of their visit, Professor Herndon felt worse than usual and found some silvery, scaly eruptions on his skin. A famed Viennese physician diagnosed the problem as a minor case of psoriasis and advised a salve of ammoniated mercury. The rash disappeared, and by the time the newlyweds had returned to Chicago, Professor Herndon felt completely normal.

His skill and reputation as a diagnostician steadily increased. By then I had started a surgical practice at the Presbyterian hospital and often asked him to help with problem patients. He always made an astute diagnosis and knew what to do for them.

A few years after his return from Vienna, he had a fine motorcar with a chauffeur. He joined the best clubs, savored expensive cigars, and grew fond of aged brandy. Despite his busy private practice, he taught students and continued his clinics at Cook County Hospital. Prairie Avenue paid for the time he spent with the poor at County.

They had no children—unusual for a Catholic family. His lively wife threw herself into social work and had lavish parties in their new home on Ashland Avenue. Her social contacts with the wealthy and influential didn't hurt Professor Herndon's practice. One evening I saw them at a concert in Exposition Hall. They were arm-in-arm, the picture of love and happiness.

It was, I think, a few years before the war when Professor Herndon had trouble concentrating on work and complained of deafness.

There were more strange symptoms, such as sudden pains in his legs, which lasted from a few moments to as long as a half an hour. At these times, he became increasingly nervous and left work to his assistant. When the pains were at their worst, he spent more time at his club and had two or possibly three brandies with lunch rather than his usual one.

One day at the hospital, he pulled me aside in a corridor. He was very agitated. Tears rolled down his face.

'My new assistant, that young fellow from the College of Physicians and Surgeons is trying to poison me.'

He wiped his eyes. I noticed the handkerchief was dirty.

'And that's not all. We can't have children because he's having an affair with my wife.'

The whole thing was so preposterous. I didn't know what to do, but said something soothing and went into a patient's room to get away.

On some days he was his old brilliant self. At a dinner to benefit the hospital, we talked about the election. Mrs. Herndon hoped Teddy would best Wilson. The Herndons were sitting next to me. He became agitated and rattled his silver fork and spoon.

'The damned meat is poisoned.'

He threw the plate on the floor and left the table.

We begged him to take a vacation or see a specialist, but he brushed off our suggestions. By that time, I had gotten on the staff at the County Hospital by giving a box of cigars to a Commissioner. I was with him at the front door of the hospital on Harrison Street, when for no reason he became enraged and began beating his Negro driver with his black bag. When I stopped him, he had a blank look and mumbled like a drunken man.

'Now, why did I do that?'

I thought he was having mental problems, but he refused to see a doctor. He ignored his wife's suggestions for a vacation in a different climate. One afternoon at the Union League Club, he had a fit. At first, there was a spasm of his right hand and foot. Then with a scream, his entire body jerked violently back and forth. He frothed at the mouth and bit his tongue until blood dribbled down his chin. He was still unconscious when friends took him home to bed.

After that episode, old reliable patients found other physicians. He stopped coming to Rush and no longer lectured. His wife stayed with him, but there were many days when she stayed in virtual seclusion. He moved out of his grand office and no longer was asked to make consultations. For several years, I occasionally saw him, a tattered derelict, clutching his black bag stumbling along the streets on the West Side. By then, his only patients were the poor prostitutes in the red light district.

He had more convulsions, and ever-longer periods of amnesia. Finally, a police wagon picked him up outside a saloon on Madison Street and took him to County Hospital.

He was strapped onto a four-wheeled cart to await his turn to be seen by the harried intern. He snored and drooled and was still drowsy when the intern came to his side. He claimed to be a physician and that his wife and assistant had poisoned him to get his money. They intern noted that the pupils of his eyes were constricted and did not react to light. There were no deep tendon reflexes in any of his extremities. One side of his face was flattened, and his once portly body was now only a frame covered with loose folds of skin.

The intern scribbled, 'psychotic reaction due to alcohol, possible stroke' on the admitting slip and sent him to the Detention Hospital for psychopathic patients at Wood and Polk Streets. Over the next few days, Professor Herndon, known in the hospital only as 'John Doe' woke up and became aware of his surroundings. For a few hours, he seemed happy, euphoric, and called to the intern and said that he was ready to make rounds.

'Where are my students?'

A while later, he looked at his fellow derelicts and searched for his black bag.

'We have some very interesting patients on the ward.'

The intern patted his arm and ordered full restraints to his arms and legs to prevent his wandering around. That night, Professor Herndon vomited, and since the leather restraints prevented him from turning over, a bit of gristle caught in his windpipe. He died alone and without identification.

One of the grand traditions of the County Hospital was the Thursday morning autopsy sessions. I always attended these sessions because there was always an interesting bit of pathology to be seen.

The body was wheeled out and dumped onto the porcelain table for dissection in front of the students and attending physicians. The 'Count,' a German who had trained in Berlin, was the head pathologist. He made a great show of an autopsy and passed the fresh organs around on trays for examination by the audience.

He habitually half-chewed, half-smoked a cigar and left the smoldering stub on the corner of the autopsy table. Most of us smoked in the morgue in an attempt to overcome the overpowering stench of all the bits of rotting flesh, old blood, and excreta which had spilled onto the floor over the years. I was in the front row with the rest of the attending doctors, but the students hung back until the last minute, then rushed in, breathing through their mouths.

The morgue attendant slid the body onto a dissecting table. It was shriveled and pale, stiff with rigor mortis, but I instantly recognized the professor. While the intern recited a short history and the physical findings, assistants made a y-shaped incision across the chest then sliced down through the abdomen. The organs were removed and laid out on metal trays. The 'Count' himself made the scalp incision and jerked back the skin exposing the skull, which he opened with a hammer and chisel. He then slid in a long blade and severed the vessels, nerves, and the spinal cord until the brain lay in his hand. He held it to the light and said, 'Ya, ya, what have we here...ya, ya, look at these theekening of the meninges and the eencreased fluid at the base of the brain.'

He then laid the brain on one of the metal trays, stripped away the meninges and sliced the gray cortex into centimeter-thick sections. He arranged the slices on the tray and with the tip of his knife pointed to a gray firm mass, an inch or so in diameter in the left cerebral hemisphere.

'Ya, ya, just as I suspected. Here is the gumma, typical of neurosyphilis.'

I stared at the brain and thought back over the twenty or so years I had known Professor Herndon. My mind went back to his vivid demonstration of the young man with a chancre in his mouth. I was certain that he had acquired syphilis from the patient.

The Count picked up his cigar, chewed a moment, then pointed with the tip of his blade to the body, now lying on the table, bereft of heart, brain, and abdominal organs, and decreed, 'Thees man lived a dissolute life.'"

"That, my young friends," Dr. Ferguson avowed, "is why I wash my hands so carefully."

DEATH OF A GENERAL

The little examining room on Ward 65 was crowded with the new patient and his visitors. Four women dressed in black, with black lace shawls over their heads prayed and wailed in Polish. Two men with faces as somber as their black suits and full of respect stood by the chipped, white-painted bed.

The patient appeared to be about seventy years old. He was handsome, even distinguished, with a large frame that nearly filled the bed. His white hair was close-cropped and he had strong features with a fine well-trimmed, tobacco-stained mustache. He occasionally moaned and muttered, "boli, boli," which I later learned was the Polish word for pain. I pushed aside the visitors and reached for his wrist, with what I hoped was a calm, reassuring touch. His hands were strong with blunt fingers. His nails were clean, but the skin was pale, dry, and hot. His pulse was rapid and weak.

The women were fat, and one had a huge, hairy mole on her cheek. The two men had erect, military bearings.

"What is the matter?" I asked.

The old man went on muttering, "boli, boli."

I tried again, this time asking one of the visitors.

"What is wrong? Why did you bring him here?"

They talked back and forth with some arm waving. The nearest man came close and whispered.

"He can't piss. We had to bring him to this hospital because there is no money."

"How long has he had trouble urinating?"

My question was met with a perplexed expression. I tried again.

"How long has he had trouble pissing?"

"He has not pissed for two days, and before that, with much trouble. The General is very important. Who will be his doctor?"

"I am the intern on-call today. I will be his doctor."

He looked at me with suspicion and seemed to know that I was only a few weeks out of medical school. He shrugged and turned out the palms of his hands. I was familiar with the gesture.

"He also has much stomach pain and will not eat his food."

I turned to the bed and commenced to take down the sheet covering his chest and abdomen. The man who spoke English gave a sharp command in Polish and waved his hand. The women filed out into the hallway and wailed even louder. There was a jagged scar across the patient's right chest and shoulder. His heart and lungs were sound. His urinary bladder was tensely distended with urine and very tender. When I felt inside his rectum, the prostate gland was large.

"How did he get the big scar?" I pointed to his chest.

The interpreter thought for the right words, then spread his hands.

"The Germans, the Germans surprised his men in the forest. They shot the General, but he lived. He saved many of our people in the villages."

I explained how the big prostate prevented him from urinating and that it was necessary to put a tube into the bladder to drain urine. I didn't know if he understood, but he talked for a long time with the General in Polish, then asked, "Will the General live?"

"Yes, of course. This is a common problem in older men. After the bladder is drained, a specialist can make a simple operation and remove the prostate."

I tried to sound professional and reassuring.

There was no nurse on the floor during the P.M. shift, but I had catheterized men in a private hospital under the watchful eye of an attending physician. I rummaged around the shelves and cabinets in the treatment room and found a foley catheter, antiseptic, towels and a pair of rubber gloves. The old man waved all of the visitors out of the room when I pulled down the sheet to put in the catheter. I held his penis with one hand and inserted the catheter. It met an obstruction and would go no further. I simply could not push it into his bladder. Every few minutes the old man moaned softly, but he did not move. My face dripped onto the sterile towels and my gloves were filled with sweat. I finally forced a smaller catheter past the obstruction. Urine flowed in a dark, steady stream into a two-liter bottle on the floor.

He gave a long sigh as the pressure was relieved. He smiled and wrung my hand.

"Dank you, dank you."

I wrote the history and physical in the ward office. When I looked in on him a half hour later, he again wrung my hand. The women were no longer wailing. They bustled about making the General more comfortable. The interpreter said that the General thanked me for making him so much better.

A couple of attendants moved him out on the crowded ward. There was no room along the walls. His bed was in the center aisle. The ward was like an oven. The July sun had beat unmercifully through the unshaded, open east-facing windows. There was only the barest breeze, and that carried the foul stockyard stench of manure and dying animals.

There were nearly a hundred old men on the ward with a variety of diseases. They had incurable cancer, heart disease, diabetes, cirrhosis of the liver, and stroke. The old man nearest to the nursing station had cancer of the lung, but he still spent most of his time rolling his own cigarettes and smoking. A half-dozen patients with tuberculosis were waiting for a place in the sanitarium. Occasionally a patient would shuffle to the bathroom. Most stayed on their thin, sagging cots and looked at peeling green paint or stared at the open windows. There was nothing to see or to cheer a sick man. They wheezed, smoked, coughed, and occasionally tried to find a more comfortable position. They suffered in the heat, and several who couldn't take liquids became dehydrated and required intravenous fluids.

After visiting hours, the Negro attendants flung supper trays onto the bedside tables. They did not stick around to help feed the men who could not reach for the plate or spoon. The meal consisted of white bread, baloney, half of a canned peach, and pitchers of Kool-Aid. It was an unappetizing meal for poor, sick old men. My new patient ignored the food. I used sign language and told him to drink lots of water. He emptied a pitcher and I got him another.

A few more patients with heat exhaustion who needed intravenous fluids came in during the night. I did not see the General again until the next morning. To my amazement, he was pale and in more pain. The catheter was filled with blood clots and his bladder was again enlarged. Another intern looked at him and asked if I had drained the bladder slowly or all of a sudden. I said that over a liter or so had drained out in about half an hour.

He shook his head.

"Jesus, Tom, when you let the urine out of a chronically distended bladder too fast, the veins rupture and bleed. All you can do now is irrigate the bladder with saline and hope the bleeding stops."

The nurse was too busy to help. The other intern showed me how to irrigate the foley catheter with a bulb syringe and saline. Several times the bag on the end of the foley catheter broke and the catheter came out. I started intravenous saline through a needle in an arm vein and by midday, he had lost so much blood he needed a transfusion.

I spent the whole, terrible day irrigating blood clots out of the foley catheter so his urine could drain properly. When I left to get more blood from the blood bank, his bladder would fill and the catheter would clot and have to be replaced.

The old man patiently endured this nightmare and only when his bladder would fill with blood would he moan, "boli, boli." All of this took place on the open ward. The other old men had their own problems and paid no attention. After three or four days, the bleeding slowed and the urine cleared.

On the morning after the bleeding stopped, he got out

of bed and carried his urine bottle to the bathroom, where he washed and shaved. That noon he ate everything on his plate. I made motions for him to drink and he emptied pitchers of water.

Two or three times a day, he wrung my hand and said, "dank you." He knew a few words and liked speaking English. I called him "General Ski."

The next Sunday afternoon, a week after he had arrived, was visitor's day. The crowd surrounding his bed included a priest who spoke English. I asked visitors to donate blood.

"Many people will give their blood for the General. He is a great hero," the priest said.

"Why is he so important?" I asked.

"The Germans took many villagers to the woods and there they would kill everyone with a machine gun. When the Germans took the men from Bochna, the General and his soldiers were hidden behind trees."

The priest pointed his finger like a pistol.

"The General killed the German squad and saved the men. When the Russians came, the General escaped to an American camp."

The priest shook my hand.

"Thank you, thank you. The General is a very important man."

I was terribly embarrassed. The other said, "dank you."

They had brought food, cigarettes, and a Polish-language newspaper. Color came back to his cheeks and he was stronger. He regularly got out of bed. The attendants gave him a pair of hospital-issue khaki pants to go with the hospital gown. He helped other patients and every day straightened out the rows of beds with military precision. He paced up and down the ward, carrying his urine bottle with his shoulders drawn back and his mustache bristling.

The urology resident saw him and agreed that he had a big prostate and needed an operation. Unfortunately, the men's urology ward was filled, and there were a dozen or so other men waiting to be transferred for surgery. He also said that he couldn't take him until the patient had a kidney X-ray.

This was a problem, because each male medicine ward was allotted only two kidney X-rays a week. My first two requests for the X-ray were lost. I hand-carried the last requisition to the X-ray department in the main building and spoke to a radiologist.

"Damn, I would like to help, but we are short on technicians. The County Board forgot to put us in the budget."

I pleaded for the old man. He said he would see what could be done. The kidney X-rays were finally done a week later.

In the meantime, he developed a high fever and had pus in his urine. The catheter had caused an infection in his bladder, which spread to the kidneys. A sulfa drug didn't work, so I gave him a new antibiotic, terramycin. The nurses gave him a couple of capsules during the day, and I arranged with the intern on-call at night to give him more.

Unfortunately, one of the side effects of terramycin was diarrhea. Four or five times a day, he picked up his urine bottle and raced to the bathroom with explosive diarrhea. Even on those trips, he squared his shoulders and walked with a military stride.

He grew weaker every day, and when he went for his kidney X-ray, the attendants left him with no food or water. He came back to the ward in the mid-afternoon of another scorching day, dehydrated and with a high fever, lying in a pool of diarrhea.

Again, he required intravenous fluids. The veins in his arms were clotted, and large bruises darkened patches on his arm where the needles had gone through the vein and fluid had run out into the tissue under his skin. He was feeble, but still squared his shoulders and each morning straightened the rows of beds with military precision.

This proud, strong old man was a shriveled shell of the patient who had come onto my ward a month ago. I felt terrible. My stupidity had caused him so much trouble, yet he still had thanked me and thought that I had treated him well. The urology resident told me that he would be operated upon the next morning.

I came back the next evening, but another patient was in his bed, and the attendant said that he had not come back from surgery.

The last time I saw the General alive, he had been transferred to the urology service. This was another large open ward. Bed against bed lined the walls. Each man had a catheter draining into a brown urine bottle. The ward smelled of stale urine and tired old men. He took my hand in both of his and said over and over, "dank you, dank you."

He looked at the uneven rows of beds, and said slowly and sadly, in broken English, "There is no discipline here."

WARD 41

"EMERGENCY, EMERGENCY, I GOT A BLEEDER," an attendant shouted. The clattering gurney left blood trailing from the corridor to the treatment room. The patient was dressed in a blood-soaked dark skirt, blouse, stockings, and high-heeled shoes. The Emergency Room had sent her directly to the ward. Her skin was deathly white. I grabbed her wrist, but couldn't find a pulse.

"My God, is she still alive?" I said.

Mrs. Lynn, an old, experienced County nurse was right there.

"Try the neck," she said.

There was a faint pulse in the carotid artery. She was alive, just barely. I made a lucky stab with a needle into a vein at her elbow and hung a bottle of normal saline.

Mrs. Lynn put shock blocks under the foot of the bed.

"Get three units of type 'O' from the bank," she said.

I ran down the hall and punched the button for the elevator. It didn't come, so I raced down four floors to the blood bank. The elevator door on the first floor was open and the operator was talking to a buddy.

"Give me three pints of 'O negative' for Ward 41," I yelled from the door of the bank.

For a change, the technician didn't argue, but took three bottles out of the refrigerator. Back on the ward, minutes later, the thousand cc's of saline had finished. I started the first pint of blood. In the meantime, Mrs. Lynn and an attendant had removed all her clothing except a black brassiere. She was a lovely girl. Her blood had soaked through the perineal pads and the sheets.

Dawkins, the obstetrics resident, arrived in a few minutes and took charge. I pumped in the blood while he stabbed at the femoral vein to get a blood sample to type and cross-match for more transfusions. He gave her a shot of ergotrate.

"Take this sample to the bank and order six more units," he said.

I dashed to the blood bank and returned with more blood. By then, her pulse was stronger and the blood pressure was nearly eighty.

The girl couldn't have been much more than twenty years old. She had long black hair, even features, and a stunning figure. Her skin had a deathly pallor, and she occasionally moaned like a wounded animal.

The name on the admitting slip was "Jane Doe." There was no history. The bleeding slowed. She came out of shock. Young people are resilient. When Dawkins palpated her distended abdomen, she moaned with pain.

"Her belly is tender. She has peritonitis," Dawkins said.

I aimed the light while he examined her with a vaginal speculum.

"Stop that, stop that," she cried.

The girl was too weak to resist. The vagina was filled with dark blood clots and yellow pus.

"It's a botched abortion. She needs an operation. Order penicillin and streptomycin and keep giving blood," Dawkins said.

She woke up and clutched my hand.

"Nick, Nick, Nick, help me."

I wondered who she was. Very few beautiful young women came to the County Hospital. Around midnight, she had another hemorrhage.

Her eyes were brittle and too bright. Her cheeks were flushed with fever and her pulse raced. The infection had spilled into her peritoneal cavity.

She looked at the blood, and at the vomit-stained green walls of the treatment room.

"Where am I?"

"The County Hospital."

Tears rolled down her cheeks. She looked into my eyes.

"Who are you?"

"The intern. What's your name?"

She sobbed and her eyes wandered over the dirty green wall.

"I'm a graduate student at the University of Chicago."

The attending surgeon came from home. We met him in the hall outside the treatment room.

"It looks like a back-alley septic abortion with a perforated uterus," Dawkins said.

Abe Berger, the attending obstetrician, was one of the best in the city. He was a handsome, stocky, middle-aged man with a neat gray mustache. Even at three in the morning, there was a flower in the buttonhole of his blue suit and a heavy gold chain across his vest. He had a great practice and rich ladies adored him. Abe examined her very gently. She winced under his delicate fingers, but didn't cry out.

"When did this happen? Who did this to you?"

She covered her face and sobbed. The nurse gave her a shot of scopolamine and morphine. We lifted her onto the gurney.

During the jolting stretcher ride to the operating room she moaned.

"It wasn't supposed to hurt. Nick paid fifty dollars."

I took her to operating room D on the seventh floor. She cried out when two nurses helped lift her from the cart to the operating table. A pretty blond nurse anesthetist clamped a mask over her face and put her to sleep with ether and oxygen. We pulled the sheet away from her naked body and one of the nurses shaved her perineal hair and put a catheter in her bladder. While I scrubbed her distended belly with soap and water, Abe and the resident were at the scrub sink, soaping and brushing their hands.

"Who is she?" Abe asked.

"We don't know her name. She won't tell us," Dawkins replied.

Abe meticulously lathered and scrubbed his strong, well-kept hands, then rinsed and went into the OR. I had already painted the belly with iodine and alcohol. The resident and nurse covered her with sterile drapes while Abe stared out the window. Obstetricians work at night and often see the sun come up. Usually their patients are happy.

Abe opened her abdomen with a neat slash. Cloudy yellow fluid and blood gushed over the drapes. He packed away the intestine and lifted the uterus out of the pelvis. It was swollen and had a ragged hole. More foul-smelling pus came from deeper in the pelvis. There was a hole in her colon. The abortionist had perforated her uterus. The instrument, perhaps a coat hanger, then went through the bowel. Abe cursed in Yiddish as he cleaned out the pus and sutured the bowel. He looked at me with brooding brown eyes.

"Talk to her and find out what sonofabitch did this," he said.

The uterus was infected and still hemorrhaging. It had to come out to save her life. She would never have babies. Abe was one of those great surgeons who instinctively knew what to do. When the uterus was in the specimen pan and the bleeding stopped, Abe scrubbed out, leaving Dawkins and me to close the wound. The operation had not lasted much more than an hour.

She was still asleep from the anesthetic when I left her in the recovery room. Abe took us across the street to the Greek restaurant for ham and eggs. I drank a lot of strong, sweet coffee and was ready for another day.

When I came back to the ward she was thrashing about and tried to get out of bed. The nurses locked her hands and feet in leather restraints. For several days, she was delirious and burned with fever. Her eyes were too bright and never seemed to close.

"I want to die," she screamed.

The nurses moved her to the darkened, dirty little side room for patients who were not expected to live. She was the sickest patient I had seen during my internship. I had to stick her veins with new needles for the intravenous glucose and saline several times a day.

On the third day after the operation, her abdominal wound was red and swollen. She screamed a long piercing animal scream when I removed the skin sutures and released a cupful of foul pus.

I spent a lot of time in her room. She moaned horribly and rolled from side to side when I tried to find a vein. Her arms were swollen and blue from the needles. Her clear white skin turned a dull yellow and her cheeks were sunken. She had diarrhea and fouled her bed. I changed her pus-soaked dressings and cleaned the wound with peroxide every day.

There was a terrible odor in her room. She lost weight and her hipbones and ribs protruded under her skin. Her eyes grew dull but they were always open, staring at the dirty green walls. This beautiful woman had become as skeletal as a Russian prisoner.

I read textbooks about wound infections and generalized sepsis. Despite new antibiotics in larger doses, her fever was a high spiky line on the chart. I gave her fresh plasma because the books said it was important to keep up the serum protein. After many tortuous days, the fever came down, and her angry red wound began to heal.

One evening during rounds, the residents and interns stopped by the foot of her bed. The resident studied the chart and examined her wound.

"Can you tell us what happened?" Dawkins asked.

She stared at the green, peeling paint on the wall.

"Do you remember the operation?"

She didn't move. The room was deathly quiet.

"You were bleeding badly and your uterus was infected. We had to take it out. You can never have children."

She did not respond. She didn't hear or was too numb to understand.

Abe came in for rounds to see patients and teach students on Friday afternoons. There was an entourage of a half-dozen junior medical students, three interns and a couple of residents. He joked with the old nurses who came along to enjoy the show.

The ward for surgical obstetrics was like all the others in the main County Hospital. It held sixty to seventy-five patients in a long room at the end of a corridor with windows on each side. There were rows of sagging, paint-chipped beds along each wall. When the ward was busy, which was most of the time, there were extra beds in the middle aisle. The nurse's station looked out on the ward. The treatment room and "side rooms" for very ill patients were along the entrance corridor. Six nurses with a few attendants looked after the ward for the entire twenty-four hour day.

The patients were young women who came to the hospital with cramps and bleeding after a miscarriage or "spontaneous" abortion. Most were the result of self-induced or "criminal" abortions, as they were called at that time. An unsterile coat hanger seemed to be the favored instrument. Others douched with bleach or other poisons which eroded the vagina. Some of these poor women died and went to a cold steel table in the morgue. The lucky ones got to County in time. They came at all hours of the day and night. The interns gave morphine, intravenous fluids, and blood if necessary. The next morning, patients were lined up to have dilatations and curettage.

In most hospitals, a trained obstetrician did this procedure with the patients under a general anesthetic. At County, there were too few anesthetists. We gave an extra large dose of morphine to the patients before the operation. The interns quickly learned how to do D & C's. It was surprising to see how well most patients recovered. Out on the ward, young women gossiped and joked with their neighbors. They seemed happy to be done with their pregnancies.

During rounds, an intern recited the history and then Abe would grill the residents about how they had handled the case. He criticized the residents in front of the whole crowd when they hadn't made the right diagnosis or had otherwise screwed up. They took it and never complained, because they respected Abe. He was skilled and honest and knew what was going on.

He stopped at the bedside of my patient and stroked his chin.

"Who did it?"

"I don't know and she won't tell us her name," I said.

She was on her side, with her back to us. Abe sat on the bed, and took her hand.

"Roll over and talk to me."

For a while she was motionless, then turned a little and looked at him out of the corner of her eye. Her hair was a black tangle. Her cheeks were sunken and smudged with deep dark circles. The room smelled and she looked like a mad woman, but with an air of tragic beauty. He put his other hand on her forehead and stroked her hair.

"You are a beautiful girl. This is not the end of the world. There is a lot to live for."

He kept stroking her forehead.

"What is your major?"

"English literature." Her voice was the merest whisper.

"Now you will understand Thomas Hardy."

Abe went on stroking her hair and she clutched his hand.

"Eat, get out of bed. You must go on with your life," he said.

Abe's face was dark and angry when we left her room. Near the end of rounds, he stared out the window and voiced resolutely, "The laws against abortion are so stupid."

Abe must have touched something deep within her soul, because the next day, she ate some of the tasteless hospital food and used the bedpan by herself. Soon, the nurses moved her to the open ward. She was in a bed halfway down the ward between two giggling Negro teenagers. I tried small talk and jokes when I changed her dressings, but was too young and awkward. She stared a long ways into space and never spoke.

Almost all of the patients had visitors on Wednesday evening and Sunday afternoon. On visitors' day, she borrowed a comb and put on some lipstick. Visitors flocked to the ward but Nick never came.

By the time I stopped by her bed again, she had signed herself out of the hospital.

A TEACHING CASE

Bill Cassaday awoke, shivering cold with no feeling in his hands and feet. He tried in vain to focus one scummy eye. The other was glued shut. There was one spot of warmth and a purring vibration under his coat. He couldn't remember where he was, or how he came to be there. As he slowly came awake, he felt the little cat that nestled against his abdomen for mutual warmth. His ribs and back hurt. When he tried to sit up, a sharp pain stabbed at his ribs. The small gray cat slipped out from under his coat, jumped over his back, and sat in the alley by a garbage can. Bill struggled to sit up and leaned against a brick wall.

A thin film of snow covered the broken bottles and garbage in the alley and the chilly November wind rustled old newspapers. He fumbled in his coat pocket for the wine bottle. It was empty and he threw it at the cat that nimbly leaped out of the way and sauntered east on Madison Street.

"Damn cat'll come back, when she's hungry."

He clutched at a drainpipe to stand. When he got over being dizzy, went through his other pockets. The welfare check was gone and only a nickel in his hip pocket.

"Son of a bitch, ain't got nothin an' I'm about froze to death. God damn, got to find a place."

The Pacific Garden Mission was a long ways away and wouldn't open until afternoon. Besides, he got pissed off at all the praying. He could sell a pint of blood and that made him think of trying to get admitted to the Hospital. He had spent almost all of one winter at the County for a hernia operation. The surgical ward was very crowded and it took a while for the interns to get around to his case. After the operation, he poked at the incision with a finger until the wound was red and drained pus. The resident blamed the interns for his infection. Bill complained of intense pain and worked on the sympathy of the young intern. He managed to stay in the hospital until warm weather.

The thought of a warm bed and enough to eat was cheering, so he staggered out of the alley and shuffled west on Madison. At the corner of Madison and Racine, he leaned against the signpost to catch his breath, then turned south and dragged one cold foot after another.

His stomach growled.

"Son a bitch, I need a drink. Gettin the goddamn shakes."

He thought about the gray cat that had shared his food and had often slept with him. She was small and often hungry and once, when he had a room, she had taken a crap in the corner. He missed her and almost turned around, but he needed a drink and a place to stay.

At Polk Street, he saw the great dome of the Greek Church, a familiar landmark, and realized that Lefty's was only a block away.

A faded sign swinging in the November wind said "Bar and Pool Hall." The greasy windows were so misted, it was hard to tell if Lefty's was open. Bill jiggled the knob and the door opened onto a long, narrow room with the bar on one side. In the back there was a jukebox, small booths, and a pool table under a single shaded light. It was too early for breakfast, and even the most hardened drinkers were still sleeping. There were smudged glasses on the bar. A little yellow light came from the kitchen.

It was a dirty little joint, but the food and beer was cheap. Medical students and interns from nearby hospitals came in the evenings to shoot pool and roll dice with the locals. They drank beer and snacked on pickled pig's feet and hard-boiled eggs fished from dirty jars. Generous portions of ravioli and spaghetti were served on most nights and on Fridays, there was fried fish. A thin-crust pizza was the house specialty. On weekends, students came for the fifty-cent breakfast of greasy eggs, bacon, toast, and coffee.

Lefty, the original proprietor, had died before the war. The current owner, Antonio Bunelli, sat on the bar stool nearest the kitchen, reading an Italian paper and drinking coffee. He was swarthy, bald and fat, with a dirty apron hanging over his gut. He didn't look up when his first customer stumbled through the door.

Spittle trickled from the side of Bill's mouth and his rheumy eyes locked onto the bottles ranked up behind the bar. He pulled himself onto the barstool nearest the door and put both elbows on the bar. He clenched his hands together to keep from shaking.

"Gimme a shot and a beer."

Tony did not stop reading, but said, "Lemme see yer money."

Bill dropped his nickel on the bar.

"There's more where that came from, now gimme the shot."

"You ain't gettin nothin with that."

"Ah, come on. I'll do the dishes tonight, just gimme a shot."

He suddenly felt dizzy and tried to swallow a wave of nausea. He clutched at the bar, turned his head and vomited a cupful of yellow bile on the floor. More dribbled down his chin onto his coat. The stench of sour vomit joined the palpable aura of stale sweat and sweet wine. The Italian flung the newspaper on the bar.

"You dirty sonabitch, get out, get out!"

The old man shrank away and whined.

"I'm a sick man. I'm on my way to the County right now. Come on, at least gimme a cup of coffee."

Down on Maxwell Street, the Jews say it's bad luck not to make a sale to the first customer of the day, so the fat Italian reluctantly waddled to the kitchen. Bill heard the sound of running water, then Tony came back with a chipped white mug a little more than half filled with weak black coffee.

"You sonabitch, you put water in the coffee. Hey, don't I get any sugar and cream?"

"Goddamn, git it yerself," Tony snarled.

Bill pulled himself down the bar, and got the cream pitcher and sugar bowl. He added two heaping spoonfuls of sugar and filled the cup with cream, stirred slowly, and drank half of the coffee. He added more sugar and cream until he had a sweet, coffee-flavored sludge, which he sipped slowly. Tony took the sugar and cream away, or he would have filled the cup again.

Bill felt better, but his hands shook so bad he could hardly hold the cup.

"Listen, buddy, gimme a shot and put it on the tab. I'll make it good."

"You scum, drunken dirty scum, you ain't paid for your last drink. Git the hell otta my place."

"You ain't gettin my business no more."

Bill slid off the barstool, went out and slammed the door.

The wind blew gusts of snow when he dodged traffic crossing Ashland Avenue. He had to sit down for a while beneath the "L" track before he could go on. At the corner of Polk and Wood, he came to the County Psych Hospital, a sooty fortress with barred windows. A couple of medical students hurried past, bent against the wind and shivering in their thin cotton hospital uniforms. He could easily fake the DT's and get into a psycho ward, but the patients were too violent. It was best to try for the main hospital. One of his buddies who knew the signs and symptoms of appendicitis had talked his way on to a surgical ward. A knife-happy intern believed the story and took out his appendix. Bill didn't like the idea of having another operation.

A medical ward would be best. The worst they could do would be to draw a lot of blood for tests and take X-rays.

He went in the main hospital through the emergency entrance off the alley, which ran from Wood Street clear through to Wolcott. A couple of cops were unloading an old lady from a paddy wagon at the back door. Inside, a Negro

clerk asked the usual bunch of prying questions, which she had
no business knowing. He gave his real name, "William Foster
Cassaday," but used an empty lot on Halsted Street for his
address. For next of kin, he said "Samantha Cat."

He sat on one of the long wooden benches in the dark
waiting room on the men's side of Admitting to wait his turn. In
a little while, a big nurse with short blue, dyed hair and a voice
like a drill sergeant came by.

She shouted, "Open your dirty mouth."

She stuck a thermometer under his tongue. Then,
waving huge tits and fat behind, went down the line of men
sitting on benches. Her starched white uniform rustled so much
you could hear her coming. When she disappeared around the
corner, Bill took out the thermometer and touched it against
the radiator. He also bit the inside of his mouth until the blood
ran. The nurse came back and jerked the thermometer out of
his mouth. She rolled it back and forth and then read 103
degrees.

"Are you shittin' me?" she yelled.

Bill had a violent fit of coughing and spit out a teaspoon
of almost pure blood. The nurse wrote "temp 103, coughing
blood, possible pneumonia" on a sheet of paper and went on to
the next man.

Bill went to the washroom and cleaned his face and
hands, then combed his hair with his fingers. He tried to scrape
the dirt and vomit off the front of his coat with a wad of wet
toilet paper. It was easier to fool the interns if you looked
respectable. The waiting room was warm, and he was very
tired. He leaned against the wall and dozed off. Bill was asleep

and missed hearing his name called the first time, so it was late afternoon when he finally saw the admitting intern.

The County interns worked twelve-hour shifts for a month in the Admitting department. It was considered a good deal because they had half a day off to catch up on sleep or to drink a few beers.

The women's side of Admitting was to the left from the back door. Most female patients were in the process of having babies, but the interns sorted out every disease known on earth on any given working day. Their job was to make a snap diagnosis and decide if the patient should be admitted to the hospital or sent out. They alternated shifts working on the women's and men's sides of the corridor.

It was a slow time of day. Patients from the morning or afternoon had been admitted to the hospital or sent to a clinic. Later in the evening as the bar room brawls heated up, there would be stab and gunshot wounds.

Tom Slocum, the admitting intern on the men's side leaned back on a plain metal chair with his feet up on a small writing desk. He was in an expansive, generous mood because in a couple of hours he had a date with a hot student nurse. After plying her with martinis at the Greek's, he planned to take her up the back stairs to his room in the intern's quarters. He was at the point in his daydream when she slipped a pink cashmere sweater over her head and generous breasts bulged out of a lacy black brassiere. The reverie broke when Bill shuffled into the dingy examining room. Tom sat up, leaned forward, and placed his elbows on the desk.

"What's the matter, Pop?"

Cassaday went into a prolonged coughing bout and spit a spoonful of blood into a bit of wadded-up toilet paper.

"I been coughin' blood and the nurse said I got a fever of a hunnert and three degrees. I got pneumony."

"Open your mouth."

The old guy's tongue was cracked and red, signs of vitamin B deficiency, and his mouth was dry. The light was so dim that the intern did not notice the bite marks.

"Open your shirt."

Cassaday fumbled with a row of buttons.

"The underwear, too."

Cassaday got the top couple of buttons undone on his long, gray underwear. Slocum put his stethoscope on Bill's skinny chest and listened to a couple of heartbeats and to the lungs for a half-dozen raspy breaths. Slocum leaned back and drummed his fingers on the metal desk.

"I'll give you a prescription for penicillin. Take a couple tablets four times a day, and stay in bed."

Bill Cassaday was alarmed.

"Doc, I ain't no bum, just down on my luck. Ain't got no place to go tonight an', here, look, I can't hardly keep my hands still. See they shake. I got pneumony bad."

Slocum sighed and thought about how the medical wards were loaded with patients and the interns were overwhelmed with work. On the other hand, the old guy did look sick and if he sent him out, he would be worse the next day.

He wrote on a slip of paper, "Admit, male medicine, pneumonia, possible TB, possible Parkinson's disease." Both diagnoses were a possibility and might keep the ward intern off his back for admitting another old crock.

An attendant took Bill to receiving, where he stripped off his tattered, wool army shirt, work pants, and underwear. These were wrapped in his black overcoat and tied into a bundle, which he would get back when he left the hospital. He then went through the "bath," after which the attendant gave him a hospital uniform, consisting of old khaki pants, held up with a string and a short white gown that tied in the back. He kept his socks, which had huge holes in both heels and at the toes, and his shoes.

A black attendant put him into a cranky wheelchair and rolled him to the elevator, down to the tunnel, and then up another elevator to Ward 65 in the male medical building.

In the ward examining room, he climbed onto a bed that had once been painted white, but was now chipped and rusted. A thin striped mattress sagged on a wire frame. Bill sighed happily. He knew this was his lucky day when a very young man, dressed in white duck pants, shirt, tie and a white coat, bustled into the examining room.

He carried a black bag and had a stethoscope draped around his neck. There was an otoscope in the breast pocket of the coat and tongue blades in his side pockets along with a flashlight, tuning fork, and reflex hammer. Walter Johnson was a third-year medical student with short brown hair, glasses, and an earnest smooth face. The regular ward intern had left him in charge of the ward while he went to dinner.

This was his first clinical rotation and he was eager to make a good impression on his intern and the attending doctor. His job was to take the history and do a physical examination on new patients. He sat down next to the bed with a clipboard on his lap, pen in hand.

"Mr. Cassaday, how old are you?"

"About 60."

"And what is your occupation?"

"I am a certified public accountant, but on account of my bad health, I ain't working."

"Mr. Cassaday, what brought you to the hospital?"

In reply, Bill went into a spasm of coughing and produced a bit of blood.

"I been doin' this now for a couple of weeks, and got the chills and fever too. My stomick hurts somethin awful."

For almost the next hour, answers followed questions until the student had written Bill's medical history, including his complaints of headache, backache, abdominal pain, occasional vomiting, and weight loss.

The history was followed by an examination, which started at the top of the head and ended with the rectum. The student used each of his new instruments to look or poke into Bills mouth, eyes, and ears. He pressed his new stethoscope against Bill's scrawny chest, listening carefully to his heart.

He dutifully recorded the first and second heart sounds and then listened to the squeaks and rattles in Bill's abused lungs. He found that the patient's liver was enlarged and that he winced and complained of pain when his upper abdomen was touched. He banged away with his reflex hammer on Bill's elbows and knees and finally, with a frown of distaste, put on a finger cot and poked his finger up Bill's rectum.

When he was done, Bill said, "Hey Doc, you sure know your stuff. Any chance ya got a smoke?"

Walter pulled a pack of Camels out of his shirt pocket and gave his patient a cigarette. Bill sucked in the smoke and inhaled gratefully. He smoked half and saved the rest for breakfast.

The intern returned from dinner belching and grumbling about liver and onions. He took a quick look at Cassaday, read the student's history and became really pissed off.

"For kee-rist sake, this guy's a wino, a dump, a crock. Why did he get admitted to my ward? They shoulda sent him back on the street or to Psych. It will take weeks to do all the tests and X-rays you want and you're gonna waste my syringes and needles drawin' blood on this crock? He even looks like he's going into the DT's. Give him a big shot of paraldehyde."

Paraldehyde smelled terrible, but it gave Bill a mild buzz and helped stopped the shakes. He had some bad dreams and trouble sleeping, but he did not go into full-blown alcoholic withdrawal. They gave him penicillin for his suspected pneumonia and powders for a possible stomach ulcer. After a few days, he felt pretty good.

County food was cold glop—white bread and cheap processed meat, but it was better than nothing. He was warm, had a bed, and his medical student kept him supplied with smokes. After a couple of days, the nurse moved him to the "up" ward, where the patients were not too sick and could get up and walk around.

Bill felt pretty good and sometimes thought about the little gray cat, which had kept him company more than once. He did occasionally have a real pain in his gut, which he figured would keep him in the hospital until the social worker sorted out his welfare checks. He helped feed other patients, and generally made himself useful while he waited for all his X-rays and tests to be completed. Walter Johnson hunted for TB bacteria in Bill's sputum and practiced drawing blood from his skinny arms.

After a couple of weeks, Bill finally went to the main building for his stomach X-rays. He waited on the benches in the X-ray department all morning, then swallowed the chalky barium. The X-rays turned out fuzzy like they had been developed in the rain.

Ed Bayne, one of the ward attending men, made rounds every Friday afternoon. He was a professor from Northwestern, a smart doctor, and a very good teacher. He wore rimless glasses, had a sharp, pinched nose, and intelligent, quick eyes. His strands of hair were left long and were combed back over his scalp, which was always darkly tanned as a result of his fishing trips out of Key West.

The interns showed him patients with puzzling diagnostic problems. He could often make a diagnosis after hearing the student recite the patient's history by standing at the foot of the bed, studying the patient's face. It was also his job to grade the medical students' histories and physicals.

He listened carefully as Walter Johnson read Bill's

history and then checked out the positive physical findings. Dr. Bayne found a spot of tenderness in Bill's upper abdomen. Walter held the X-rays up against the window and pointed to a suspicious area in the stomach.

Dr. Bayne stroked his chin and studied the films.

"Could be an old ulcer or an early cancer."

He turned to the student.

"What would you do now?"

Walter had not expected the question and didn't know what to say, so the intern chimed in.

"I think he needs an operation. The surgeons can biopsy the stomach and take it out if it's cancer?"

Dr. Bayne chuckled.

"Yes, and you could transfer him off the ward. Why not send him to Snyder for gastroscopy? He can look into the stomach and take a biopsy without an operation."

A gastroscope is a long, wicked, hollow tube, lighted at one end. It is inserted into the mouth of the patient, passed down the esophagus and into the stomach. A skillful operator can get the instrument into the stomach and see its lining, but with considerable discomfort to the patient. For a while, they had paid derelicts to allow the procedure to be done, but nobody had ever had a gastroscopy twice. It was a lot like swallowing a sword.

On the day when Bill was scheduled to have the test, Dr. Snyder was conducting a graduate school class in the use of the instrument. He had demonstrated the procedure, and now it was the student's turn.

A middle-aged doctor from Omaha, Nebraska, who wanted to be a specialist in gastroenterology, did the gastroscopy on Bill. He had watched the procedure several times and did not think that it looked too hard.

Bill was groggy after a shot of morphine, and his mouth and throat were numb from a cocaine spray. He did as he was told and laid down on the table, with his head well back. He opened his mouth as instructed, but commenced to struggle when the doctor put the instrument in his mouth.

The doctor was angry and pushed harder on the scope.

"Hold still."

The student had trouble getting the scope past Bill's throat, but Dr. Snyder was lecturing to other students and did not pay much attention.

Finally, with a vigorous shove, the student pushed the scope into what he hoped was the esophagus. Bill felt a severe crushing pain in his left chest. He struggled so much that the alarmed doctor removed the scope. There was blood on the tip of the instrument.

The pain became much worse. Back on Ward 65, the intern gave Bill morphine and thought that he was having a heart attack. He called a resident, who brought an EKG machine from another ward. The EKG tracing did look abnormal.

"Yeah, it looks like a coronary. Give him morphine and oxygen and keep him in bed," the resident said.

Bill was in agony for two days, then drifted in and out of a coma. Just before he died, he asked a nurse to look after a cat and wondered if he could have a drink.

At the autopsy, the pathologist said the cause of death was a torn esophagus. There were also old scars on his lung and early cirrhosis of the liver. All of the students and interns learned a great deal from the case. Down on Madison Street, no one missed Bill except a small gray cat.

A COLD CHINAMAN

"He's the coldest damn Chinaman we've seen all night. The little sucker was in a snow-drift behind a restaurant up on Clark Street," said the first cop. The two bundled-up beefy police officers laughed as if finding an iceman was the funniest thing that had happened on their shift.

Tom Slocum, the emergency room intern, went out to the paddy wagon. At first, he thought the little Chinaman was dead. He put his stethoscope on the man's cold chest and listened closely. There was a distant, slow heartbeat. The man was cold as ice, and his hands and feet were deep blue.

The attendants put him on a cart and rolled him into the County emergency room. They stripped off his ragged T-shirt, cotton pants, and tennis shoes.

It was a little after midnight. Slocum, the admitting intern on the men's side, had sent a stream of tired old men to the medical wards. They had a variety of diagnoses, but mostly they wanted a warm place to sleep. He would normally have sent the Chinaman to medicine, but the medical wards were packed with twice as many patients as bed spaces. Instead, he looked at the patient's blue, ice-cold legs and diagnosed frostbite. He admitted him to a surgery ward. Frostbite could lead to gangrene, and it was often necessary to amputate a foot or leg.

He had no identification. The clerk entered him on the County records as "John Doe" and sent him to Ward 54, the next male ward in the rotation.

It was simply bad luck that Jake Isaacs was the intern on-call that night. When the nurse called, he was in bed reading a medical journal.

Jake was a slender, balding studious veteran of the Korean War who had graduated at the top of his class from Chicago Medical School. He had been accepted for a residency at Mayo and at the Massachusetts General Hospital. These were top-notch residencies, but the County internship promised a wealth of experience that private hospitals couldn't provide.

Jake was older than most students and wanted more responsibility for his patients. He was married and had a small son. Everyone respected him because he was hard-working and methodical. In a few years, we thought he would be a great diagnostician. He was an all-around good guy who went out of his way to help old geezers with their multiple problems.

Most interns would have grumbled about getting out of bed to see one more elderly patient with frostbite. Jake didn't complain. He put the Chinaman in a warm room next to a radiator and did a complete physical examination.

The patient was a skinny little man of indeterminate age. He had wispy, gray hair and a stringy little beard. His skin was yellow and dry as parchment paper. Except for being cold, he looked fairly healthy.

There was one surprise finding. The old Chinaman had an enormous scrotum, which transilluminated with a flashlight. There was fluid around the testicle, a typical hydrocele, and not a hernia or tumor. It was not dangerous. Most men had them operated upon because they could be painful and were a nuisance. Jake started an intravenous solution of glucose, wrapped him in blankets, and had the nurses place hot water bottles on his abdomen.

The next morning, the Chinaman was not only awake, but also sitting up in bed, chattering in Chinese. There were no signs of frostbite, much to everyone's amazement. Within a couple of days, he was wandering around the ward, holding the hospital issue khaki pants around his skinny little waist. He caused no trouble, and pretty soon, everyone called him "John Chinaman." The hydrocele made a noticeable bulge in his pants.

"Me fukkee two, me fukkee two," he said, every time a nurse went past his bed. He said this so often, the nurses decided that his name was actually Fukei Tu. His name was changed from "John Doe" in the ward record book.

He remained sprightly and cheerful, except at mealtime, when he contemptuously waved aside most of the cold, unappetizing food served by the County Hospital. One night when rice was on the menu, he rolled the rice into balls and shoveled the food into his mouth with his hands. He then settled back on his bed and belched contentedly. Jake ordered a rice diet for him. After eating his rice, "John" leaned back, clutched his scrotum, and smiled.

"Me fukkee two, me fukkee two."

The male surgical wards were always busy. There were gunshot and stab wounds, peptic ulcers, and old men with cancer. Many patients had gangrene of their legs due to poor circulation, aggravated by the cold weather. Leg amputations were common, and so a lot of old men spent their days in a wheelchair. Men with hernias and other simple problems came for their operations during the winter so they could get in out of the cold. They didn't mind the sagging beds, crowded wards, and lack of privacy.

We three interns were always busy changing dressings, starting intravenous fluids, and running to the blood bank for transfusions. There were never enough nurses to do the routine chores. We took call for new patients every third night and assisted in the operating room until late afternoon. We could barely keep up with the work. On our nights off, we drank beer at the Greek's or dated nurses.

Jake Isaac went home to a small apartment to eat and sleep on his nights off. Sometimes, when he wasn't too tired, Jake played with his new son. In those days, interns only made $25 a month. His wife Rebecca worked as a part-time schoolteacher. They were looking forward to July and a medical residency.

The ward resident, Jim Bromfield, did all the surgery for the ward, and was night surgeon for the whole hospital every fourth night. He was always tired and left the running of the ward to us interns. It was almost a week before he got around to see the Chinaman.

When Jim stopped at his bed with us interns, the Chinaman fondled his scrotum.

"Me fukkee two, me fukkee two," he said.

"That sucker must hurt. Have you asked him if he wants it fixed?" Jim inquired.

"He doesn't speak English, and he never complains. In fact, he seems kinda proud of his scrotum," Jake said.

The rest of us interns examined the enlarged scrotum. Jim explained how to make the diagnosis of a hydrocele.

"Get Tommy Chenn, the anesthesia resident," he said.

Tommy Chenn's family were wealthy Mandarins from Hong Kong. He didn't recognize the little man's dialect.

"I don't know what he's saying, but it sounds like he has three balls and makes love to two women a night. I really think he's a little crazy," Tommy said.

Jim saw him again on rounds and decided to operate.

Jake had no luck with finding another Chinese interpreter. The ward social worker said he was probably an illegal immigrant. A lot of them washed dishes in the high-class restaurants downtown.

Jake tried to explain the operation with sign language and had the old man scrawl an 'X' on the surgical permission form. Two days later, we took him to the operating room. The Chinaman laughed and chattered all the way to surgery. He looked about the operating room and quickly went to sleep with intravenous Pentothal. The operation was simple. Jim Bromfield sutured a small hernia and removed the hydrocele sac.

The next day, Jake was busy and didn't make rounds on his patients until mid-afternoon. The little Chinaman was sitting up in bed with his pants pulled down, frowning at the neat row of stitches and his shriveled scrotum. Instead of being grateful and friendly, he snarled and shook his fist at Jake. He sulked and hissed Chinese epithets at the nurses.

When the weather warmed, the ward gradually emptied

as the men who had come to the hospital to get out of the cold decided to leave. The ward social worker arranged for the little Chinaman to go on welfare and found a room for him in a cheap hotel run by a Chinese landlord. The wound healed perfectly. The ward nurse, a true saint, found new clothing and arranged a taxi to take him to the hotel on a Friday morning.

A week or so later, we were standing around the ward office waiting to make rounds when the little Chinaman walked up the corridor. This was not surprising, since patients often returned to their wards to see old friends or to have their prescriptions for medicines renewed.

He walked past the other interns and turned towards Jake.

"Me no fukkee two," he screamed.

With one surreal motion, he drew a long butcher knife out of his jacket and thrust the knife in an upward arc. The blade entered Jake's upper abdomen, went through the liver and then sliced the left ventricle. Jake didn't have time to put up his hands or to step back. Before the Chinaman had pulled out the blade, Jake slumped to the floor with blood pouring out of the wound. For a moment, Jake looked about the ward with stunned, disbelieving eyes, and then died. Jim Bromfield tackled the Chinaman and wrestled him to the floor.

"You sonabitch, me no fukkee two, me no fukkee two," said the Chinaman.

The cops had been right. He was one damn cold-blooded Chinaman.

A LONG WAIT

The boy was slender and small for his age. His skin was a light mocha, his hair was black and kinky, and his eyes were troubled. He was too sick to leave the small, hot, third floor apartment. He felt tired and threw up. His right side hurt all the time. "Auntie" thought he had the flu and gave him a tablespoon of castor oil and a Carter's pill.

That afternoon, when "Auntie" left for work, he was very hot and thirsty. He dragged himself to the bathroom to get a cool rag for his face. The mirror reflected a dirty yellow color in the whites of his eyes and sunken cheeks. The cool cloth felt good. He splashed cold water over his chest.

On the way back to the couch, he heard noises in the alley. Two neighbor boys were trying to catch the big ginger tomcat that lived in the empty building next door. The old cat had a torn ear and his tail had been burned. He scampered down the alley followed by shouts and pieces of broken brick. No one was playing stickball. It was too hot.

The boy felt sick again and spit up a half cupful of bitter yellow fluid. He lay down on the couch and waited for his "Auntie."

She was not really his aunt, but his grandmother who had looked after him ever since his mother had run away with a white trumpet player. People at church whispered that the white man was his father.

"Auntie" was in that indeterminate age between forty and sixty. Her thickset body, lined face, and thin, kinky, gray hair had changed little over the years. Her hands were gnarled and painful, and she wheezed in the sultry, humid air. On work days, she wore a shapeless dark blue dress and sturdy, black men's shoes. On Sunday, she dressed up in a white blouse and skirt, topped off with a straw hat and a white ribbon.

That day, she fanned herself and waited in bright sunshine for a bus at the corner of 79th Street. The dust, whirling on a hot wind, the stockyard stench, and the diesel fumes made her wheezing worse. She took one bus to State Street, and another to the loop.

From the stop at Madison, she walked to LaSalle and went into a tall, dirty, gray building. She got off on the 12th floor and went in the service entrance to Winston, Oglethorpe, McDonald, and Kennedy. Most of the lawyers had left, but a few secretaries clattered away at typewriters. They paid no attention as "Auntie" opened her closet, put a gray apron over her blue dress, and got out her broom, bucket, and mop.

She swept up the scraps of paper, cigarette butts, and remnants of lunch. When she finished sweeping and had emptied the waste baskets, she sat on a stool in front of her closet, had a pork sandwich and some leftover brackish coffee. She then filled her bucket with water, added a cup of liquid soap, and swished gray water over the tile floor. She wrung out the mop with the roller on the bucket and went over the floor with the dry mop. It was necessary to go around the edges of the floor on her hands and knees to clean scum and dirt from the corners. She finished at eleven o'clock, turned out the lights, and dozed her way home on the State and 79th Street buses.

It was still hot when she wheezed her way up the darkened stairway to her third floor apartment. The boy was curled on the couch, with a dribble of vomit on his chin. She roused him and saw the dirty yellow of his eyes. His forehead was hot and dry. She made him drink a half cup of water and bathed his face with a wet cloth.

"Oh Lordy, he's worse. I'll have to carry him out to the County."

She got him down the stairs and to the corner, where he slumped beneath the streetlight. The bus took them to Ashland Avenue, where they sat on a curb and waited, it seemed, for hours. After a long streetcar ride to Harrison, she carried him in her arms to the Cook County Hospital.

The pediatric admitting room was down a flight of stairs, off the alley, which ran between the main hospital and the children's building. A clerk wrote names on a sheet of paper, and then parents and patients waited to see an intern. One elderly nurse checked older children for pubic hair. At the slightest sign of sexual maturity, the child was sent to the adult examining room in the main building. Along the sides were small examining rooms, separated from the waiting room with a cloth curtain. Each room had a desk and chair for the doctor and a table for the child.

Admitting was always crowded with tired, sweating mothers and their sick, crying, snotty-nosed babies. In winter time, a cold draft poured over naked babies each time the outside door was opened. Now, during the hottest days of late June, the room was airless and suffocating. The average wait to see a physician was usually six hours. During epidemics, the time could be longer. In the winter, there were colds and pneumonia. With the onset of hot weather, hundreds of babies had diarrhea and vomiting. Families who could not afford refrigerators left bottles of milk to cool on windowsills. The milk spoiled on the first warm days of spring. There were always children with broken bones, burns, fevers, tuberculosis, and worms. Patients with measles or chicken pox waited in the same room, infecting others.

On this particular hot night, the Filipino resident left shortly after midnight, leaving the night intern, Tom Slocum, to see the remaining patients. He had already spent a full day on Ward 36, the diarrhea ward. There had been twenty new babies, all squirting liquid stools and dehydrated almost to the point of death.

The ward was terribly overcrowded and smelled horrible. Three of us interns and a resident spent the day drawing blood for chemical studies and starting intravenous fluids. It was neverending because often, no sooner than an IV was started, the baby or an inexperienced aide would pull it out. There were never enough nurses or supplies. That particular day, three infants on the ward had died from malnutrition and dehydration.

It was near the end of his internship. Slocum was very thin and had dark circles under both eyes. His last pair of white duck pants was splattered with blood and dried diarrhea stools.

Sometime after three in the morning, after he had seen and examined the last of the waiting patients, he rubbed the stubble on his chin and stumbled into a linen closet and lay down on wheeled stretcher. It was very hot, and his eyes were gritty, but after twisting and turning and wadding up a sheet for a pillow he dozed off for a few minutes. The Negro aide shook his shoulder.

"Docta, they is a new patient."

He rubbed his eyes and stumbled half-asleep into the waiting room. An old Negro woman sat on the wooden bench, a small boy sprawled across her lap.

Slocum waved towards the small curtained examining room.

"In here."

The old woman picked up the boy in her arms and went into the examining room. She laid the boy on the wooden examining table.

Slocum slumped into a chair at the desk and rubbed his eyes.

"What's wrong?"

"He thrown up everything and his eyes turned yeller."

"Anything else?"

"He ain't want to do nothing an he won't eat."

Slocum turned the chair around and leaned close to the boy. The sclera of the boy's eyes were a deep yellow, and his skin was hot and dry. He ran his hand over the boy's abdomen down to the bone of the iliac crest and, pushing deep with his fingers, found the edge of the liver. It was enlarged and the boy winced and cried out when he touched it. The liver was enlarged and very tender.

"Has his urine turned color?"

The old lady shook her head and didn't answer.

"Brown, dark brown," the boy whispered.

"How long has he been sick?"

"'Bout a week."

At that, Slocum felt a hot rush of anger, which he knew deep down was irrational and stupid.

"Then why did you bring him here in the middle of the night?" Slocum shouted.

He had the silly idea that the old woman had brought the boy to the emergency room to make his life miserable. He scribbled a few lines on the admitting sheet.

"This isn't an emergency. Take him on home and come back tomorrow during regular hours. He has hepatitis."

He abruptly stumbled back to the cart and laid down. The little room was scorching hot and airless. He was too agitated to sleep. In a little while, the day shift nurses arrived. Slocum got up, stretched, and walked down the alley behind the main hospital to the intern's quarters. There was a little breeze, and the alley was almost cool. He took a long, cold shower, put on a clean shirt, then went to the cafeteria for some toast and greasy scrambled eggs.

After a couple of cups of sweet black coffee he felt better. There was still an hour to go on his night shift and so he went back to pediatric admitting. The same old lady was sitting on the middle bench. Her back was straight and the boy was lying down with his head on her lap. Slocum was surprised to see them again.

"You came back early."

The old lady raised her dark, white-rimmed eyes. She had a look of complete resignation.

"We ain't never went home."

Slocum took them back into the same small examining room and asked a few more questions. He listened to the boy's heart and lungs and felt his neck. He wrote up the history and physical examination in a nearly illegible scrawl and went to find a syringe and needle. The boy put out his arm and didn't move when Slocum jabbed the needle into a vein for a blood sample.

He looked again at the old lady. She sat ramrod straight on the metal chair with her hands folded in her lap. She wore a large straw hat with a bunch of artificial flowers in the brim. The boy wore a clean, white shirt and dark blue trousers, which were only a little dusty at the cuffs. Slocum wondered if they were wearing their Sunday clothing. Many patients put on their best clothes to come to the hospital.

"Why didn't you bring him in earlier?"

"Doctor, I din't think he was so bad until I got home from scrubbin floors downtown. We had to ride the cars to git out here."

Slocum covered his face with his hands and felt a black cloud of depression. He realized that he had done a stupid and cruel thing by making the old lady and the boy wait on the hard, backless bench.

The next day, he visited the boy on Ward 26. His thin, dark body rested on a white sheet, with his arm stretched out with a tube for intravenous dextrose. The walls of the room were painted green. No pictures, television, books, or radio was there to cheer the boy. Slocum felt a terrible sense of shame and wanted somehow to make it up to him.

"How are you?"

Slocum tried to be cheerful, but the boy turned his head away and lay very still. He said nothing.

SHIP'S CAT

Two aircraft carriers, a cruiser, destroyers and a half-dozen support vessels rolled on the cold, gray sea between mainland China and Taiwan. It was the beginning of the cold war when the Reds threatened to invade tiny specks of rock, the islands of Quemoy and Matsu. The north wind blowing over the flight deck was even colder than the war. The aircraft spotters were bundled up in flight jackets and thick helmets.

The Seventh Fleet cruised the Straits of Taiwan as a part of the grand Cold War strategy dreamed up by our obstinate politicians. By midmorning, the last of the big A-1 Skyraiders were launched and disappeared into the overcast sky for the morning patrol. According to prevailing scuttlebutt, they carried atomic weapons. The USS Hancock, CVA 19, secured from flight operations by midmorning. During morning sick call, while I was examining a sailor, a corpsman burst into the examining room.

"Doc, the bridge got a communication from the Belatrix. They need a Medical Officer."

The Belatrix, a general cargo ship, had a Chief Hospital Corpsman but no doctor. I was the Junior Medical Officer, not long out of an internship. The Senior Medical Officer, an old regular, told me to get ready. I told the corpsman to have the patients return at evening sick call and borrowed a warm flight jacket.

By the time I got up to the hangar deck and walked through the parked aircraft, the Hancock slowed to a steady ten knots. The Belatrix came alongside on a parallel course a hundred feet away. The bosun's mates were rigging the transfer line amid the usual bunch of off-duty sailors who were clustered around hoping to see some fun. I had treated most of them for one thing or another, mostly athlete's foot and clap.

"Hey Doc, you gonna get your ass wetter'n hell."

They laughed, and I was worried. Occasionally during a high line transfer, the basket dipped into the sea. One could easily get more than a wet rear end.

I put on a life vest and climbed into the basket held steady by a bosun's mate. Sailors on the other side heaved on a cable. The basket was attached to a highline with a pulley arrangement. Sailors on the Belatrix pulled on another rope and suddenly I was away from the hangar deck and over the open water. There were whitecaps on very angry-looking waves. The basket dipped, but never touched water. I swayed and dipped like a carnival ride at the county fair. It was really sort of a fun ride. Within seconds, a burly, grinning Chief helped me onto the deck of the Belatrix.

"Welcome aboard, Doc."

The Belatrix carried everything from fresh vegetables to spare parts. Her only armament was a battery of old three-inch anti-aircraft guns. Her decks were covered with loading cranes and winches for the transfer of supplies. Only a few days before, she had sent the frozen turkeys, hams, fresh fruit, and vegetables for the Hancock's Christmas dinner.

The fleet cargo ships had the best of everything when it came to food and supplies. The men and officers who clustered around the highline winch laughed and joked. The deck officers wore sweaters with open collars and some of the men had flapping shirttails.

It was all different on the carrier. Our skipper insisted on spit and polish and ran a tight ship. He was bucking for Admiral. Officers wore ties and compulsively shined their shoes to a high polish. An enlisted man caught with his shirttail out was sent to the Captain's mast for punishment. I was slovenly by Navy standards, but the Captain could do little to punish a two-year Medical Reserve Officer.

The Chief Hospital Corpsman who met me on the deck had a deeply tanned, lined face and his dark hair was tinged with gray. From the row of hash marks on his sleeve, he was an old Navy man. He put out a hand.

"Welcome aboard sir, Chief Daniels."

"I'm Dr. Slocum. What's up?"

He led the way down a ladder to a clean, gray-painted passage going aft.

"I think this man has appendicitis and needs an operation," he said.

In the passageway, several sailors gave way to let us pass. They touched their hats and nodded to the Chief.

"Morning, Doc."

The crew seemed to like him. On a ship this size, the Chief Corpsman treated ailing sailors. Most of the Chiefs knew as much about common medical problems as the doctors. Many of the sailors trusted them more than they did medical officers.

A watertight door labeled with a red cross led to a spotlessly clean, quiet corridor with doors leading to a treatment room and a small office with neat, gray, government-issue desks. It was a typical ship's sickbay. The Chief explained that the treatment room doubled as an operating theater. Behind the treatment room was a ward containing twelve bunk beds for inpatients. During wartime, a ship this size would have a Medical Officer.

The sick sailor lay very still in the first bunk with a bottle of saline hooked up to his right arm. He was a young gunner's mate with an anchor tattooed on his forearm.

"Moore came to sickbay yesterday with what looked like a touch of the flu. He had vomited once and felt nauseated. I gave him Phenobarbital with belladonna and excused him from work. Last night he came back with belly pain, which got worse this morning."

The Chief's clinical description of the man's symptoms was very professional. I stooped over the bunk with the feeling that I might be in over my head. The patient was about twenty years old, slender with red hair. His cheeks were a bit sunken and his mouth was set in a hard painful line. His pulse was a touch faster than normal. His skin was warm and dry.

"Hi. Show me where it hurts," I said.

Moore pointed to his right side. "Right here. It's worse when I move."

I felt his abdomen. When I pressed low over the right side his face contorted with pain.

"Jesus, Doc, that hurts like hell."

"He vomited a couple of times last night and had a fever," the Chief said.

"Yeah, it looks like appendicitis. He needs an operation. Why don't we just transfer him to the Hancock?"

"His appendix might rupture during the transfer. That highline wouldn't do him any good either. The second-class corpsman is a trained operating room tech and we have all the instruments. The OR can be ready in half an hour. Do you need anything special?" the Chief asked.

I was on the spot. There didn't seem to be a choice. The man needed an operation, but I was a year out of internship and not a qualified surgeon. I had watched the residents do appendectomies at the Cook County Hospital and had done a couple more onboard the Hancock with the Senior Medical Officer. It is a pretty routine operation in a well-equipped hospital.

It would be necessary to do a spinal anesthetic and if the ship rolled, the drug could either go up the spinal canal to the brain and cause total paralysis, or it might not work at all. I had done a lot of spinal taps, but only a couple of anesthetics.

We could have given him a big dose of antibiotics and transferred him to the Hancock, which had a much better-equipped sickbay and a regular operating room. Instead, because I was young and dumb, I decided to go ahead. It would be about like doing kitchen table surgery in the backwoods.

"OK, let's do it," I said.

I wrote a note on the medical record and ordered an injection of morphine. The Chief and I changed out of our uniforms into white scrub suits. The patient was becoming drowsy from the morphine when two corpsmen rolled him into the makeshift operating room. The officer of the deck kept in touch by the ship's telephone and brought the ship to a new course. The engine's vibrations dropped and she barely rolled. There was no excuse. I had to go ahead with the anesthetic.

The ampoules of tetracaine, ephedrine, and glucose were neatly done up in a sterile pack. I pulled on sterile gloves while the corpsmen turned Moore onto his side. He groaned a little when I inserted the long needle into his back.

It was a lucky shot because spinal fluid immediately dripped out of the needle. I injected the anesthetic and within a few minutes, Moore was numb up to his ribcage and couldn't move his legs. The OR tech already had the instruments and sutures arranged on a table covered with a sterile sheet. I scrubbed up at the sink and dried my hands on a sterile towel. The OR tech held out a sterile gown.

"Thank you," I said.

The familiar ritual of scrubbing, gowning, and pulling on sterile rubber gloves was soothing, and I felt a real surge of confidence. Another corpsman had painted the patient's belly with an antiseptic and covered him with sterile sheets. He then went to the head of the table and checked the patient's pulse and blood pressure. These guys were well-trained and knew their job.

The patient was slender. That made the job a lot easier. There is nothing worse than slicing through a slippery layer of fat. I measured the distance from the belly button to the anterior spine of the ileum and put one finger on the spot, which was two-thirds of the distance from the umbilicus. Every medical student learns that the appendix is located at "McBurney's point"—usually.

I was determined to look good and laid the knife down hard to make a real incision, not just a scratch. Chief Daniels caught the bleeders with a hemostat when I cut through the skin and muscles. Fortunately, he knew what he was doing. I separated the muscles with the tip of a hemostat and one finger, just like the residents did back at the County Hospital. Then, I poked two army-navy retractors between the muscles and gave them to the Chief to hold while I opened the peritoneum.

There was a little cloudy fluid in the peritoneal cavity. It looked like we had made the right diagnosis. I was high with excitement and at the same time beset with anxiety. I prayed to whatever deity might listen that the appendix would be in the right place and not behind the cecum or deep in the pelvis. With one finger, I felt inside the abdomen. There were loops of intestine and the pouchy cecum. It was all warm, moist, and mostly everything felt the same.

Suddenly I touched a ropy, firm structure. It was the appendix. Eureka! It was red and swollen and easily flipped out of the peritoneal cavity. Luckily, it was in the right place and hadn't ruptured. After a couple of ligatures to the artery and the base of the appendix, I cut it out and tossed it into the basin.

"Chief, you made a good diagnosis. Congratulations!" I said.

We stitched the wound, and I was ready to relax. Someone telephoned the bridge that the operation was over. It had taken a little over an hour. I was smart enough to realize that the whole thing was due to dumb luck rather than skill. It could easily have been a disaster.

I was writing orders for antibiotics and more IV fluids when the Chief came into the office.

"Doc, it's lunchtime. How do you like your steak?"

"Medium rare, but I have to get back to the Hancock."

"Shucks, Doc, there's plenty of time. The boys are fixin' chow for you right now."

"OK, I guess a few more minutes won't hurt anything," I answered.

By the time we had Moore settled back in his bunk, a corpsman brought a covered tray.

It was spectacular. The juicy, perfectly-grilled tenderloin steak was on a crisp, toasted bun with crunchy French-fried potatoes. There was coffee and a huge wedge of apple pie with ice cream. I hadn't seen such good food since the last time we had liberty in Yokuska.

"Ya want another piece of pie, Doc?"

I thought a bit and checked the time.

"Sure, I can make room for another small piece. Say, this coffee is really good."

The Chief was hovering around like a hen with chicks.

"I added just a touch of medicinal brandy, seeing as how you have had a tough day. By the way, we need your advice on another little problem."

It was getting on three o'clock.

"I really have to get back to the Hancock, or I'll be AWOL."

The Chief shook his head.

"They just started afternoon flight operations and can't rig a highline until all the planes have landed."

We went back to the treatment room where a huge, completely bald Chief Petty Officer clutched a cardboard box.

He had sagging blue jowls and broken veins on his nose. Gray hair spilled out of his open shirt, and hash marks lined up halfway down his sleeve. He was the Chief Master-at-arms, with nearly thirty years of service. His gut sagged over his belt. Scars crisscrossed his baldhead. He had broken up more than one bar fight.

"Chief Lublinski, here's the Doc from the Hancock," the Chief Corpsman said.

The Chief Master-at-arms glared. His voice was a low growl.

"Know anything about cats?"

Pride prevented a truthful answer.

"A little," I said.

He gently placed the cardboard box, lined with a regulation navy wool shirt, on the treatment table. Inside was a pitiful little gray and black cat. Her forlorn face looked like a black mask for a formal ball. She mewed pitifully. The huge Chief stroked her fur and made meowing noises.

"Somethin's got to be done. I can't stand it if anything happens to Lulu."

The little cat had dull, dark, sunken eyes. She was panting and her ribs stuck out under ragged fur. Her head rested in the Chief's huge hand.

I figured this was some kind of a joke. They wouldn't really ask me to treat a cat. The big Chief was serious, and it seemed better to go along and see what happened.

"How long has she been this way?"

"She's always thrown up a little, but it got worse last week. All she can keep down is a spoonful of water."

I was at a loss for words. It was just too bizarre. It was against Navy regulations to have pets onboard ships, and here was a Chief Master-at-arms, who was charged with maintaining discipline, harboring a cat.

The corpsman came to my rescue.

"We gave her penicillin yesterday. Do you think another dose would help?"

"Sure, can't hurt anything," I replied.

"She ain't taken a crap for a couple of days. How about a little cascara?"

"That might be alright," I said.

"Do you think she needs vitamins?" the Chief asked.

"Wouldn't hurt," I mumbled.

The Chief gently stroked the cat's ears.

"I dunno what could be wrong. I give her pieces of steak in fresh milk. She gets an egg every week."

I stalled for time to think, but didn't come up with anything.

"How long you had her?" I asked.

"I found her in an alley behind a whorehouse in Tijuana, about a year ago. She was a little thing, crying like a baby. I just couldn't leave her. We'd had a bit to drink and just for the hell of it, I sneaked her onboard ship under my shirt."

He belched and scratched his chest.

"She stays in the Chief's quarters. None of the officers even know she's onboard. We sometimes take her on deck, back on the fantail when there ain't no officers around."

Her fur was thin in patches, especially on her shoulder.

"What's wrong with her fur?"

"I dunno. She licks herself all day."

The cat coughed, then gagged and brought up a teaspoonful of yellow liquid.

The Chief cradled and rocked her in his arms.

"Poor Lulu, poor Lulu."

The treatment room was crowded with hospital corpsmen and a couple of Master-at-arms petty officers.

"Got any ideas, Doc?"

I shook my head.

"My aunt had an old yellow cat that threw up. The vet said he had hairballs and gave him mineral oil," one of the corpsman said.

All of a sudden, I remembered a five-year-old kid who had been a patient on the pediatric ward at the County Hospital. She had a big lump in her belly that everyone thought was cancer. One day an older doctor came by and noticed the bare patches on her scalp. He diagnosed a hairball in the stomach. The kid admitted that she had been pulling out her hair and then swallowing it. The surgeons operated and took out the hairball. She was fine after the operation.

"Put Lulu on the table," I said.

The Chief gently put Lulu down.

"Don't hurt her."

She lay on her side with her head down. The tip of her tail twitched. The fur on her abdomen was a lovely pale orange, but her belly was swollen. I made a show of being a doctor and felt her abdomen. It seemed firm to the touch. I tried listening to her chest with a stethoscope. She had a strong heart, but there was a lot of gurgling in her abdomen. I had only heard bowel sounds like that in a patient with an intestinal obstruction. It dawned on me that if the cat was a human, she would have an intestinal obstruction.

I folded the stethoscope and put it back in my pocket.

The big Chief hitched up his pants.

"Well, Doc, whatcha think? You gotta do something for Lulu."

"Maybe you could take her to a vet the next time you are in port," I said.

"She won't last that long. If you kin fix humans, ya oughtta be able to take care of cats," the Chief growled.

I had dissected a cat during a physiology course in college and there really wasn't much difference in anatomy. The cat probably needed an operation, but the whole episode was getting out of hand. I had the feeling that if I didn't do something for the cat, I might not get off the Belatrix alive. It was illegal to have pets onboard a ship anyway. Drinking medicinal brandy was also against Navy regulation. The Chief Corpsman and the big Master-at-arms had planned the whole thing. I had visions of a court-martial. The Captain would yank off my insignia in front of the whole ship's company on the flight deck.

The cat moaned again. I buried my face in both hands but couldn't see a way out.

"Oh Christ, OK, let's give it a try, but no promises."

The big Chief beamed with pleasure.

"That's the stuff, Doc."

The corpsman injected a mixture of saline and glucose under her skin while Chief Daniels set out the instruments and sterile towels. The Belatrix corpsmen were getting a lot of OR experience that day.

The little cat mewed pitifully while we tied her legs to the edge of the table. A corpsman held a gauze compress soaked in ether over her face. She stopped meowing and relaxed. We painted her abdomen with an antiseptic and covered her with sterile towels.

I again pulled on a sterile gown and gloves. The whole thing was totally crazy. I made a small incision down the middle of her abdomen. There was very little bleeding. The cat's intestine was shriveled and seemed to be normal. I felt around the peritoneal cavity with a gloved finger and found a hard mass in the stomach. I was sweating and nervous, but made an incision in its wall. There was a mass of hair mixed with mucous and bits of wool which extended from the stomach down into the small bowel. I pulled out the mess and tossed it on the instrument table, then closed the hole in the stomach with a few silk stitches. It took only a few more minutes to suture the abdominal incision. We held our breath until Lulu gave a low meow and opened her eyes.

Chief Lublinski wrung my hand, and tears actually glinted in his eyes.

"Thanks, Doc. I won't ever forget this. If you ever git in trouble, just let me know. I kin fix anything in this Navy."

By then, the Hancock had secured from afternoon flight operations and the highline transfer was ready. The cluster of sailors on the Belatrix's deck seemed unusually friendly as Chief Lublinski personally helped me get into the breeches buoy.

The next day there was a radio message from the skipper of the Belatrix:

"We appreciate the services of your Medical Officer. Moore and Lulu recovering nicely."

THE SECRET OF MOOSE CREEK

When I was the night surgeon, we got a head start on the evening's work by walking through the emergency room right after the evening meal. We looked for people with abdominal pain who might have a perforated ulcer, an acute gallbladder attack or appendicitis.

If things were quiet, the junior resident made rounds on all the wards, while I had an hour or so of sleep.

Later, when the bar fights started, there would always be stab and gunshot wounds. On most nights there would be three or four cases. Most were routine operations, but sometimes there were really bizarre surgical problems.

One night a man came to the emergency room claiming that he had a coke bottle in his rectum. Sure enough, his X-ray demonstrated the bottle. Another time, I operated on a man who had swallowed an open pocketknife on a bet. There was always a great "high" when doing surgery and we never tired of operating.

As I remember, the junior resident was Jim Baker, a real nice guy and a hardworking resident. We had no more walked into the ER when a police paddy wagon rolled up to the back door.

The cops brought in a big muscular Negro man with a butcher knife sticking out of his upper abdomen. The blade was in all the way to the wooden handle.

The police had first taken him to Passavant, but the jerks over there sent him on to County without even starting an

IV. The Northwestern guys were too high-class and wouldn't treat people who did not have money.

The stabbing had happened a couple of hours before. He was drunk and scared, but in surprisingly good shape. Fortunately, the blade had not gone upward, or it would have hit the heart and killed him.

The ER intern started a saline IV and drew some blood for a transfusion, in case there was a lot of bleeding when we pulled out the knife in the operating room. There was no other surgery going on, so Baker and another intern wheeled him to the elevator and up to the eighth floor operating room.

They were still rolling down the hall when another paddy wagon pulled up with an old man, whom the cops had picked up at the Pacific Garden Mission. The new patient had a bushy, salt-and-pepper beard, and long, nearly white hair. He was unconscious and his eyes were sunken from dehydration.

I hung around to see what was wrong. One intern removed his filthy black overcoat and struggled to take down the blue bib overall held together with brass hooks and buttons. He finally got down to gray long underwear with a drop-seat. It was the kind country boys put on in the fall and took off in the spring. The patient and his clothing reeked of sour wine, vomit, sweat, and dead fish.

The intern shook the old man's shoulder and leaned close to his ear.

"Hey, Pop, wake up. What's wrong?" he asked.

The old boy moaned a little and tried to roll off the stretcher.

A note from the mission nurse said he had been complaining of a stomachache and hadn't eaten anything for several days. One of the officers said he and some buddies were drinking cheap wine when he vomited and collapsed on Lake Street.

The first intern was a high-type Harvard sort of guy. There was usually about one intern a year from an east coast school who "slummed" at the Cook County Hospital. Disgust with the lesser members of the human race was written all over his face.

"Ah, he's just another old wino with a bad liver and DT's. Send him to psycho."

The other intern, who had examined the old man, stroked his chin and seemed more thoughtful.

"I dunno. His belly is distended and there aren't any bowel sounds; could be a perforated ulcer," he said.

While the interns argued, I took a look at the old guy. His radial pulse, hard to find under the ends of the underwear, was fast and fluttery. He was breathing fast and each breath started with a long raspy gurgle. There was a lot of half-dried mucous in the back of his throat. The second intern was right. His belly was distended.

When I felt around his abdomen he moaned and tried to push my hand away.

"Ah, ah, yi, yi, yi," he muttered.

Things didn't look good. Something in his belly had perforated causing peritonitis. He was in shock and looked more like a candidate for the morgue than the operating room.

The interns cut away his underwear with a big pair of bandage scissors and covered him with a blanket. His face had a brown leathery look as if he had spent a lot of time outdoors. His skin under the long underwear was pale white and streaked with dirt.

He moaned when I pushed on his abdomen, especially on the lower, right side.

"Ah, yi, yi, yi, Jesus Christ," he said.

He had what we called at County an acute abdomen or "hot belly." This meant that something was wrong inside the belly, which needed an operation. There could be anything from a perforated ulcer to gangrenous intestine or appendicitis. There were also rare things like swallowed bones that worked their way out of the gut. Opening up an acute abdomen was like opening a Christmas package. It was always exciting and you never knew what was inside.

This was one of those cases when you could never be certain of the diagnosis until the belly was opened. One of the old surgeons who lectured the interns on acute abdomens had a lot of aphorisms.

"If you don't know, bet on the appendix. You will be right most of the time."

So I bet on the appendix mostly because he seemed more tender in the lower right side of his abdomen over the appendix.

The interns were earnest and trying hard, so I said, "It is probably a ruptured appendix because he hurts more in the right lower quadrant. Give him a couple of bottles of saline with glucose, plasma, and antibiotics. If he gets better, we will take him to the OR."

They were all ready in the operating room with the stab wound when I arrived. A pint of blood was running into an IV in his arm and his blood pressure and pulse were not bad. The blade had gone in just above his belly button and angled to the left. It went through a bit of liver, hit the stomach, and had nicked the spleen.

It took a couple of hours to sew up the holes and stop the bleeding. Later, when he had sobered up and was better, he admitted that he had cheated on his wife, and she had stabbed him.

It was near midnight when I went back to the ER. The old boy's pulse was slower, the blood pressure was up and his color was better. The interns had done a good job. His breathing was easier because they had sucked the mucous out of his throat.

"Take him to the OR," I said.

The intern pushed the cart off the elevator and into OR three, the one next to the nurse's desk, which had a fine view of the city. I loved working there at night. The nurses and aides were still cleaning up after the last case, and the anesthetist was eating a sandwich in the office. When we lifted him onto the OR table, he groaned.

"Sumbitch, take it easy. My belly hurts awful."

"Don't worry old-timer. You will be OK," I said, but not with a lot of confidence. He was pretty sick.

He squinted at the big round light above the table.

"What you aim to do, young fella?"

"You got a busted appendix and a belly full of pus. Got to operate, clean up your insides," I said.

"Yeah, yeah, I knowed something was wrong."

The anesthetist flounced in the room and fussed with her equipment. She gave him a shot of morphine and atropine. The nurses were taking their time. They worked eight-hour shifts and were never in a hurry.

"Where are you from, old-timer?"

He hesitated a moment and grunted, "Minnysota."

"Yeah, where in Minnesota?"

"Tofte," he said.

The morphine loosened him up like a couple of stiff drinks. He began a long rambling story...

"My name be Arne Severson. I be Norwegian and my people always fish in Superior, one big damn lake. Den, I go in the army and fight with the Japs. Den, when I come home to the big lake, dem eels come and take all the fish. Da nets come in empty. Ain't no more big trout. Da bank take the boat, the nets, evryting we got. Da brothers, they try cutting trees and make lumber, but dat don't work long.

"I shoot the deer and the moose for meat, but the wardens, they catch me and take my gun so all I got is to take the sports to the leetle cricks to fish for the trout. I got mad at one of them sports and quit, then went to Duluth, den, I heard they had jobs in Chicago. This bad place—too big, much noise.

I drink the muscatel—good, sweet wine. Makes me feel good. I got a little room on Madison Street but dere's rats."

"Do you have a job?" I asked.

"Sure, sure ting, I got job cleaning da fish in da market. Not always. Sometimes dere's no fish, then no work."

He closed his eyes and stopped talking. He looked pretty worn out. The nurses still weren't ready to start. I knew the area on the north shore of Lake Superior where he had lived. It is a beautiful, wild place with lots of little trout streams running out of the hills into the big lake.

"I used to go up on the Gunflint Trail with my Dad. We caught trout on the Poplar River and shot grouse with an old single-shot .22 pistol," I said.

It was nearly two in the morning. The interns were tired and wanted sleep. The nurses were still fooling around. It took a long time to sterilize and set up the instruments.

The snotty blond nurse anesthetist strolled in the room and jammed the anesthesia mask over the old guy's face. He tried to sit up.

"Dammit. Breathe the gas," she said.

The old guy struggled and pulled at the mask. She took it away from his face.

"Listen Doc, I gotta tell ya something. Hold on a minute. Gimme a pencil and paper."

I tore a sheet from the back of his hospital chart and gave him my pen, an old Parker. The anesthetist was pissed and made a couple of remarks about filthy old men and boy surgeons. The old guy's hand wavered over the paper.

"I ain't never been this sick, but you been nice and I got to tell this to someone."

He gripped the pen and jerked at the intravenous tubing. He drew a crude map.

"This here X is where the Caribou Trail comes into Tofte."

I nodded.

"You go up the trail towards Ely, about eight miles until you come to the county road. It's mostly dirt, but some gravel. It ain't too bad. Go exactly two and a half miles and watch for a big old birch tree with a blaze about six feet up. It might be all growed up. There's an old loggin' road goin' back in the bush on the right side. A regular car can get over it in dry weather. Drive a couple of miles till it gets all boggy and then go on foot until you hear the water. It's Moose Creek. Go about a mile upstream till you come to a beaver dam."

The interns were drying their hands on sterile towels, and the nurses had the instruments ready. The old guy gripped my arm and whispered.

"They's native speckled trout in the beaver pond as long as your arm. They ain't those damn sewer trout from the hatchery, but real natives. No one ever goes in there but me. I never took the sports back to Moose Crick. It's my secret place. You go on up there, Doc. I know you kin ketch big damn trout."

He groaned, lay back on the table and peacefully closed his eyes. The anesthetist clamped the mask over his face and started the ether. He was asleep by the time I finished scrubbing.

There were a couple of pints of foul green pus in his belly. I sucked out the pus, and then hunted around with two fingers for the appendix. It was red, hot, swollen like a sausage, and at the tip, there was a hole the size of a nickel.

The interns held the incision open with retractors while I fished out the appendix, cleaned up the mess and stuffed a couple of drains up under the liver. I let one of them close the incision while I shucked off my gown and gloves.

It was still black night outside when we finished, but there were lovely twinkly lights on the buildings down in the loop. I could even see the flashing light on top of the Allerton Hotel. There were no more cases, so I got a few hours of sleep before the next morning's surgery began.

I didn't see him again until late that afternoon. The interns had given him more antibiotics, a blood transfusion, and intravenous fluids and had put tubes into his bladder and stomach. His eyes were sunken. He continually pulled at the blanket with trembling fingers.

I didn't blame the nurses for putting him into one of the dismal little side rooms for terminal cancer patients. Green paint peeled off the walls, and very little light came through the sooty window. The accumulated stench of urine, vomit, and feces from previous patients hung over the room. His fever was high. It looked like the old boy was going to die.

On the third day, I removed the drains and changed the pus-soaked dressing. He was in roaring delirium tremens and had pulled out his intravenous needles. The interns had strapped him down, put the IV's back in and gave him big doses of paraldehyde. He settled down and slept for a while.

I was on-call again and came back to see him several times during the night. Once, he had a long conversation with a foxhole buddy, and then he tried to claw away the restraints and get out of bed. His eyes popped out and he screamed.

"Ray, Ray, you crazy sonofabitch, get your head down. Those yellow bastards will kill you."

He sobbed for a while and cussed a game warden named "Big Red." The next day, he was almost rational. The DT's lasted a couple more days. One night the nurse found him with his hand stretched out through the bed rails.

He stroked the air and crooned in a low voice. She tried to get him to take his medicine.

"Can't I even pet my dog? You wimmin are all alike. Old Blacky ain't messin up nothing. Why can't I keep him in the house? He's the best damn duck dog on the north shore."

He went on stroking the ears of a great black Labrador retriever until he fell asleep.

Much to our surprise, he improved after that. The nurses moved him out to the main ward with all the other old men. There were fifty beds in long rows. His place was near a window on the west side where he could look out on wet, gray March days and see old sooty snow still piled on the curbs.

His wound was better, and the dressings were no longer soaked with pus. He drank the weak coffee and took some of the tasteless hospital food. After a while, he spent his days on the enclosed sun porch in a wheelchair. His eyes were most often on the gray Chicago sky and depressing rows of rooftops and dirty, slushy streets. No one visited and he didn't talk with the other men.

One day a social worker came to see him. She arranged for a room in a flophouse hotel and made sure that he got his pension check. She also gave him some loose change so he could buy tobacco.

A couple of days before he was to go home, I made rounds with the three ward interns and a couple of students. He squinted at us and seemed suspicious, almost hostile. His intern removed the dressing. The wound was almost completely healed.

"You can go home now," the intern said.

Arne rolled a cigarette with Bull Durham tobacco. He asked for a match.

"That was a tough time. I liked to cash in my chips. I seen snakes afore, and had the shakes, but that was the worst nightmare I ever had. I dreamed I told some damfool doctor about my best fishin creek and he went and writ it up in one o'them sportin magazines."

THE WAGES OF SIN

The skin on the girl's chest and arms was charred down to muscle after her nightgown had caught fire from a space heater. She was only five years old. This was at least the twentieth trip she had made to the operating room for debridements and skin grafts because deep infections had prevented healing.

Tom Slocum teased another postage stamp size bit of skin onto the beefy red granulation tissue then held it in place with a 5-0 catgut suture. He straightened and turned away from the operating table. His glasses were fogged and sweat dripped from his forehead.

"Angelique, wipe my forehead before it drips on the wound."

The little Filipino nurse was trying to swat a fly that had entered the operating room through an open window. It was one of those days when August seemed to stretch halfway into September. She finally nailed the fly and wiped Tom's forehead with a cool damp towel. It felt really good.

"Before I forget," she said, "there is a new consult for you from Ward 36."

"Yeah, what is it?"

He reached for a new piece of skin from a saline soaked gauze pad, then slid it into place on the girl's chest.

"Baby girl Scroggins, possible pyloric stenosis. The intern is Rowley."

She taped a slip of paper with the baby's name and ward number to the door of the OR.

"Great! Call him back and say I will be there when this case is finished, half an hour at most."

Slocum felt a rush of excitement. He was a third year surgical resident and hungry for a good case. So far on pediatric surgery he had operated on burns, infected wounds, and a few hernias. It was interesting, hard work but not very challenging.

Pyloric stenosis was caused by a thickened muscle that obstructed the stomach in babies a month to six weeks old. It caused forceful vomiting, dehydration, and eventual starvation. Unlike most diseases that caused vomiting, these infants were voraciously hungry and would suck at a bottle after vomiting. Skilled pediatricians could feel the thickened muscle through the abdominal wall. It felt like a cocktail olive.

Pyloric stenosis was a classic pediatric condition, easily cured with an operation when the diagnosis was made early. Unfortunately, by the time many of these infants got to a surgeon they were starved for nutrition.

Slocum had seen the operation performed several times and had studied the Ramstedt technique named for the German surgeon who had stumbled upon the operation in the early 1900s.

With half his mind on doing the skin graft, he reviewed what he had read in articles and textbooks. One problem was wound healing and according to the latest textbook, the best incision was transverse, through the oblique muscles, much like an appendectomy incision, only higher on the abdomen. That was what he would use, Slocum thought. The thickened muscle was cut and then spread apart down to the mucosa.

The entire operation would last scarcely more than twenty minutes. Within a day or two, the baby could take her feedings without vomiting. The prompt recovery and cure was almost miraculous. It was just the sort of case that made surgery so interesting and rewarding.

He adjusted the last skin graft, inserted three more sutures, and tied the knots. Slocum covered the grafts with strips of Vaseline gauze while the intern wrapped her thin body with yards of bandage until she looked like a little mummy. He stepped back from the operating table, shucked off his gloves, and waited for the girl to wake up from the ether anesthetic. She made mewling noises and gripped his hand as she woke from the ether fog.

"Stay with her, check the vital signs, and write orders. I'll go see the consult on 36," Slocum said to the intern.

"OK, Tom."

He ran down the five flights of stairs and into the main corridor of Ward 36. Not only was there the prospect of a challenging case, but also, he had his eye on a cute student nurse who had worked on the surgical floor but moved on to babies. She was one of the students from Iowa who stayed six months at County, just long enough for fun, but then left before things got too serious.

Most of the Iowa nurses were hefty farmgirls, but this one was slender as a birch tree and had hair the color of corn shucks in October. Slocum had been changing a dressing on the ward when she tried to move a six-year-old boy out of his bed onto a cart to go to the operating room. The kid held on to the bed, kicking and screaming.

"I don' want my privates cut on," he yelled.

Slocum laughed out loud at her efforts to get the boy onto the cart and then tried to sneak a look at her cleavage. Slocum was a little over six feet tall and slender with light brown hair. Most of the nurses thought he was not bad looking.

"Hey, Blondie, how would you like to go over to the Greek's for a drink when you get off tonight?"

The girl didn't answer but wrestled the boy out of bed and on to the cart. She covered him with a sheet and strapped him in. As she wheeled the cart out the door she turned and glared at Slocum.

"I have heard all about you surgical residents," she said.

He opened the door from the stairwell to the corridor and was met with the overpowering smell of diarrhea, vomit, and stale urine.

A series of rooms divided into cubicles came off the corridor and each cubicle was jammed with cribs containing babies sick with everything from meningitis to scurvy. The most common problem was diarrhea because so few families had refrigeration for milk.

Slocum picked his way past cribs, nurses, medical students, and harried interns to the ward office. The clerk didn't know anything about patient Scroggins but said the intern on-call was in the treatment room with a new baby.

Rowley, the intern, had curly black hair, a square jaw and usually carried a lopsided roguish smile. He was wearing a crisp white uniform and looked like the reincarnation of Young

Dr. Kildare. The student nurse who was helping him start an IV seemed to think so, too. He was sitting next to the treatment table and she leaned over so that her breast touched his shoulder. Slocum took in the romantic tableau. She was the babe from the surgical ward. Then he saw the baby and forgot about the nurse.

The kid was near death from dehydration, worse than any of the abandoned orphans he had seen in Korea. The white skin of the emaciated baby was stretched on tiny bones like tissue paper over the balsa frame of a model airplane. Her dull eyes were sunken into deep sockets and she didn't whimper when Rowley jabbed a thread-like vein with an IV needle. His handsome face was set in a dark scowl.

"I can get the needle in the vein, but when the fluid goes in the vein balloons out and ruptures," he said.

There were puffy areas on her arms, where the IV fluid had extravasated under her skin.

"She needs a cutdown." Slocum said.

He felt for a pulse at her wrist, couldn't feel anything but cool, dry skin and then put his fingers on her neck, feeling for a carotid pulse. It was faint and too fast to count. The intern and the pretty student stood by while Slocum examined the baby.

"Dammit," he yelled, "she needs a cutdown, don't you understand English? Get the instruments."

Their mouths opened, but neither the intern nor the nurse moved.

"Are you deaf or stupid? Didn't you hear? Get a cutdown set," Slocum yelled.

The student covered her face with both hands and ran out of the room.

"You didn't have to yell and swear," Rowley said.

Slocum had a hair-trigger temper, and he always instantly regretted what he had said. She returned with the tray of instruments and removed the sterile wrapper. Slocum found a pair of size seven gloves in a drawer, pulled them on and sorted the scissors, scalpel, and hemostats on the sterile towel.

"4-0 catgut," he said.

He held out a gauze sponge.

"Pour some iodine on this, please."

He slopped the iodine on the baby's groin.

"Need a number 11 blade," he said.

The nurse scurried out of the room again and returned with the foil-wrapped blade. She dropped the pointed scalpel blade on the sterile towel and Slocum fitted it into the handle.

"Rowley, fill a couple 20 cc syringes with sterile normal saline."

He sat down by the table and picked up the scalpel, then made a half-inch incision in the baby's groin. There was no bleeding from the skin, a bad sign. Slocum spread the subcutaneous tissue and then snipped through more layers with scissors.

He paused for a moment to think about the anatomy.

Nerve, artery, vein, empty space, was the mnemonic which students recited to remember the relationships of the femoral artery, vein, and nerve. The damn incision was too high.

He wanted the saphenous vein where it emptied into the femoral. The veins were tiny and collapsed. It would be easy to mistake a nerve for a vein and leave the kid with a paralyzed leg, even if she lived. He spread through bits of connective tissue a little lower and found a tiny thread, which was in the right place for the saphenous vein. He tied it with the 4-0 catgut ligature.

The instruments and his fingers felt ridiculously large as he worked on the miniscule anatomy. He selected the smallest plastic catheter on the tray and then made a nick in the vein with the eleven blade. A drop of blood oozed out of the vein. It couldn't be a nerve. He picked up the cut edge of the vein with forceps and slid the catheter into the vein. There was a slow return of dark, thick blood.

"Gimme a syringe of saline."

He injected the saline while watching the vein. It worked. The vein did not rupture, so he stitched the incision while Rowley connected the catheter to IV tubing.

He stood and stretched his tense muscles.

"What makes you think she has pyloric stenosis?"

"She has been vomiting all her food and I think there is a mass in the upper abdomen," Rowley said.

Slocum looked at the baby again. Almost 50 cc of the saline had run into her vein. Her color was a little better and she seemed more alert. The abdominal wall was so thin he could see loops of intestine, like writhing snakes, just beneath the skin. It was sunken and the skin was loose. He gently ran two fingers over the surface of her abdominal wall. When he touched her, the baby opened her mouth and made a high-pitched, pitiful noise like a baby rabbit.

Beneath the edge of her liver there was a small smooth knob. It might be a pyloric mass, but it was more lateral, like a kidney. He felt again, but couldn't be sure.

It also bothered him that the baby was a girl. Most patients with pyloric stenosis were boys. It was an inherited disease. He felt a wave of disappointment. This kid probably didn't have a pyloric, so no operation would be necessary.

"I'm not so sure this is a pyloric. What is the history?"

"I told you, she vomits everything. If you want, go talk to her mother. She's out in the hall," Rowley said.

The girl, sitting on the wooden bench, leaned forward with her arms resting on her thighs. Beside her was a brown paper shopping bag. She had the soft fatness that comes from eating greasy food and not enough vitamins. Her mousy brown hair was tangled and she wore a shapeless purple housedress, men's work shoes and dirty white athletic socks.

Slocum thought she was asleep, but her dull eyes were open. She stared at scraps of cast-off adhesive tape, candy wrappers, and a bloody gauze pad on the floor. He sat on the bench next to her.

"Mrs. Scroggins, can I talk to you about the baby?"

She raised her pale, placid face, and for a moment he didn't know if she had heard or understand what he had said. After a long pause, she opened her mouth and Slocum could see that her upper front teeth were missing.

"Ah'm Bertha. Miz Scroggins is ma. Ah reckon you kin talk," she said.

"How long has your baby been sick?"

There was another long pause as if both thought and speech were hard for her numb brain.

"She allwis been poorly. Ain't never been right."

"What's been the problem?"

"Did'n wanna eat nothin."

"Did you take her to a doctor?"

She shuffled through the shopping bag until she found an envelope. The paper in the envelope was from the Mountain Nursing Service.

"Mebbe you kin read from this paper," she said.

The penciled note described how to make formula from canned Carnation milk, water, and corn syrup. There was also an appointment with a doctor at a clinic in Spring Lick, Kentucky.

"What did the doctor say?"

"Never did get to see the doctor."

"Why not?"

"It was Daddy. He beat me and threw me outen the house. He said ah is wicked an ain't nothin' but a Jezebel."

Slocum was tired and frustrated. It was long past lunchtime.

"Did she vomit the formula?"

"Never got to try no formula. Daddy threw me out."

"What did you feed her?"

"The same stuff I eats."

"What's that?"

"Most anythin', pieces of hot dog, chips, bread soaked in water or pop."

"You can't feed a baby like that. Why didn't you get formula for her?"

"Been on the road. Ain't no formula in them bus stops. Say, you know ennyone named Billy Joe? He's my boyfran."

"Look, I'm trying to find out if your baby vomited. You know, did she throw up her food?"

"Sometimes she threw up. Mostly she don't eat nothin'. What about Billy Joe? I come all this way lookin for my boyfran. He say he's a goin' in the navy an he was goin' to a camp on sum big lake up around Chicago. Then he say they was goin to send him to Californy an' I could come out to Californy when he got there. I alwas wanted ta see Californy, where they make them movies."

"Please, this is important. Your baby might need an operation. Can't you tell me if she vomited? You must have given her milk sometime?"

The girl stared at the bloody bit of gauze on the floor.

Greengold, the chief pediatrician, his back stiff with arthritis, came off the elevator. He nodded to Slocum and appraised the girl on the bench with a quick glance, then went into the treatment room.

"Been hard, walkin an' travellin with the baby and all. The lady what give me a ride to Owensboro bought some milk for her. The bottles run out afore I got here. She give me money for bus fare too."

"But, did the baby throw up the milk?"

"Ah guess, a little, but mainly she wouldna take it at all."

Slocum shook his head and went into the treatment room to see what Greengold thought about the baby.

The chief of pediatrics was an old-timer who had seen every disease in the book. He ran his fingers over the sunken soft spot on top of the baby's head, then picked up a bit of skin and finally let his fingers wander over the sunken abdominal wall. He put the earpieces of a stethoscope that hung around his neck into place and listened to the baby's chest. He shook his head and the corners of his mouth drooped.

"Some rales in the lungs and she is terribly dehydrated. What is the history?"

He looked to Rowley for an answer.

The intern ran his hand through his hair and shuffled a little.

"Kid vomits everything. She has a mass. I think she has a pyloric," Rowley said.

Greengold grimaced and felt the abdomen once again.

"No, this is the kidney, not a pyloric. She has pneumonia and is badly dehydrated. Has she made any urine?"

Rowley shook his head.

Slocum repeated the mother's story. Dr. Greengold rubbed his lower back and sighed.

"Poor kid."

He held the baby's tiny hand and studied the wizened palm.

"Poor little baby, didn't have a chance. Give her penicillin, more saline with glucose and some blood. If she makes urine, she might live."

Greengold stroked his chin and looked at the baby for a long time, as if he were trying to think of something else to do. After a few minutes, he shook his head and left. Slocum followed him out of the treatment room. The mother was still on the bench, hands on her thighs as before. She looked at him through heavy-lidded, half-shut eyes.

"My baby ain't goin to live."

Slocum sat beside her but didn't know what to say. Parents were usually hopeful and looked for reassurance. She was as placid as before and had simply made a statement in the same tone of voice she might have used to talk about the weather.

"Why did you say that? She has a pretty good chance of making it," Slocum said.

"My daddy, he say what I done with Billy Joe was sinful and someone had to die, cuz he say the wages of sin is death."

Slocum had no answer. He got up and slowly took the stairs to the surgical ward to make rounds with the interns. Afterwards, he went back to the baby's ward.

The girl on the bench with the paper shopping bag was gone. In the treatment room, the student nurse with hair like sun-ripened corn was swaddling the minikin, skeletal body with a white muslin shroud. She was sobbing.

She wiped her eyes and glared at Slocum. Her mouth was twisted with anger, as if she blamed him for the baby's death.

"You bastard. You didn't have to be so mean."

Slocum wanted to tell her not to become emotional about patients, or even handsome interns, but then, she would have to find out for herself. He had learned to stay detached from senseless death in a tent hospital with a dirt floor. He checked his watch. It was a few minutes before six. There was still time at the Greek's for a half-price double martini, or maybe two.

THE HAND

My MG, the balky English roadster, never started during wet weather, and that morning it had rained. I was late for morning rounds. The junior resident, Jim Ott, and the three interns had seen the patients, written orders, and generally had things under control. I met them at the scrub sink in the operating room.

"Anything new or serious last night?" I asked.

"There were a couple of elective hernias and one man with a burned hand," the on-call intern said.

The burn did not sound serious, and I wouldn't think about it until later.

We scrubbed up for the first case, a gastric resection for an ulcer, and when that was done, there was a gall bladder. Both cases went well and we were done in time for lunch. Then, I had a long outpatient clinic and didn't get back to the ward until late afternoon, for evening rounds.

A few ladies were recovering from hernia or gallbladder operations and another was just getting over an exploration for cancer of the ovary. They had some post-op pain and had not started to eat solid food. I patted them and exclaimed how well they looked.

"Mrs. Jones, you look so good today. Tonight, you can have some Jell-O and in a day or so, you can go home," I would say.

I was practicing a bedside manner because in a couple of months I would be out in practice.

I was upset over an infected hernia wound which wouldn't heal, but there was nothing terribly important until we came to the man with the burned hand.

He was in bed with his wrapped, right hand elevated on a couple of pillows. His dark, unkempt hair was streaked with gray. I suppose he was in his mid-fifties. He was tall, very slender, almost gaunt, and not particularly muscular. His face was handsome, but there were dark circles and deep worry lines around his eyes. His mouth was set in a hard line. His name on the bedside tag was Giovani, Robert.

"Mr. Giovani, I'm Dr. Slocum, the senior resident. How are you?"

He did not look up.

"OK."

"Are you having much pain in your hand?"

"No."

I turned to the intern.

"How did it happen?"

"He said he burned it on a stove."

"Let's take a look," I said.

The intern pulled on a pair of sterile rubber gloves, unwrapped the clean white bandage and removed the four-by-four gauze pads from between his fingers and both sides of his hand. The last layer was a strip of Vaseline gauze.

I must have sucked in a breath and said, "My god," or something to that effect. It was purely involuntary. The hand looked nothing like a hand, but a claw. The skin was burned to a leathery brown back to his wrist joint. The discoloration stopped there, just as if he was wearing a leather glove. The fingers were held, rigidly extended straight out from his hand and their tips were as crisp as burned steak.

"It doesn't hurt?"

"No."

"Try moving your fingers," I instructed him.

There may have been a twitch in his thumb and I thought his ring finger moved a fraction of an inch. The leathery skin and the lack of pain and movement were certainly indications that this was a full-thickness, third-degree burn.

"Are you sure you burned this on a stove?"

"Yeah."

I didn't notice until later, but according to the chart, a private surgeon, an associate of Dr. Meyer, the Surgeon-in-chief, had sent him to the County.

The hand is one of the most complex, wonderful structures in the human body. It takes several weeks to learn the hundreds of bones, tendons, tissue layers, and nerves of this marvelous instrument. The hand is really an extension of the brain and responsible for man's rapid evolution.

In medical school, I had dissected a couple of hands and had learned the lovely Latin names, *flexor digiti quinti*, *abductor pollicis brevis*, and the lumbricals, tiny "worm" muscles which flexed the fingers on the metacarpal joints. The tendons originated from muscles in the forearm and slid through delicate lubricated membranes.

I thought of these things while looking at the burned hand. At that time, I was a hopeless optimist and thought that all things could be cured, or at least helped with surgery. I knew so little of the harsh reality of disease, or men. It should be possible, I thought, to remove the burned tissue and cover the hand and fingers with skin grafts. I should have known better.

At that time, the usual treatment for burns was to wait for the dead tissue to slough away, then clean the wound and apply skin grafts. Recently the literature had suggested the process could be speeded up with early debridement and skin grafting to decrease scar tissue.

That night, I called Bill Stromberg, one of the best hand surgeons in the city. He saw the patient the next day and agreed that we should go ahead with early surgery. I told Mr. Giovani what we had decided.

"OK," he said.

I was beginning to think that Mr. Giovani had a very limited vocabulary. He did not look like an out-and-out bum or an alcoholic, but clearly, he was down on his luck. I asked several more times how he could have burned his hand so badly.

"On a stove," he said.

I assumed that he had been half-anesthetized by booze or drugs.

Mr. Giovani was the last case on a Friday afternoon. The nurse anesthetist put him to sleep. We scrubbed the hand and his arm with soap and water and placed it on sterile sheets.

Dr. Stromberg indicated for me to go ahead. I cut away the dead skin with a scalpel and scissors. I went to the first layer, the fascia beneath the skin, but there was no sign of bleeding or healthy tissue. The small muscles in the palm of the hand appeared to be necrotic. I didn't know what to do next.

"Better stop here and use saline dressing. See what happens," Dr. Stromberg said.

During the next week, we took him back to the operating room at least three times. Dr. Stromberg took time from his private practice to be there for every session.

Miss "G," the head nurse in the operating room, was interested in the case. She fussed with the sterile drapes and watched every scalpel cut. Miss "G" thought residents were good only to clean the operating rooms between cases. She rigidly rationed sutures and cut off the operating time on a whim. She was a whiny old maid, and we had been in a state of open warfare for a couple of years. Most residents were afraid of her because she reported every misstep to the Chief.

We carefully removed more dead, burned tissue. First, there were the thin fascial membranes, then some muscle, and finally we were down to the flexor tendons. I hoped that by some miracle, we could lay the skin grafts over the tendons and get some function out of the hand. By this time, the tips of the fingers were shriveled and black. I amputated back to the second joint.

On the ward, I helped the intern with every dressing change, adjusted his antibiotics, and looked for any sign of healing. This meant spending a lot of time with Mr. Giovani. It became clear, even to me, that he would lose several fingers. I hoped that we could save the thumb and at least one finger.

He never looked at his hand. It was almost as if it no longer belonged to him. I tried to communicate and be sympathetic, but he would not even talk about the weather. There were never any visitors at his bedside, and he had no contact with the other patients. He learned to eat with his left hand. One day, I asked how he was getting along.

"Hard to wipe my ass with the left hand," he said.

The tendons were dead and the exposed bones were dark brown. Dr. Stromberg said it was time to take the hand off at the wrist.

There was healthy tissue at the wrist joint. Vessels in the skin bled freely, and the tendons were healthy and slid easily through their sheaths. I clamped and tied the radial and ulnar arteries, then sawed through the bone just above the joint. When the intern sutured the skin over the bones, the stump looked pretty good, but it was just a stump.

I felt sad because it seemed like a personal defeat. I had wanted to save at least a part of the hand. Miss "G" hovered around the operating room during the entire case. She watched closely, and I detected a softening in her attitude.

"You tried hard. No one could have saved that hand," she said.

The intern discharged him a few days later. I wasn't on the ward when he left.

A week later in the clinic, I didn't recognize him. His hair was slicked back and he was dressed in a fashionable light gray double-breasted suit. He wore a tie with a stickpin, cufflinks, and a gold watch on his left wrist. I was astonished, because I had thought he was down and out.

"You really look good, Mr. Giovani. Looks like you can afford to pay your hospital bill."

I blurted it out without thinking, as a joke. No one ever paid the County Hospital. There probably was not even a billing department.

He sat down and rested his right arm on a low table while I unwound the bandage and removed the dressings. The wound was clean. The intern removed the nylon sutures and re-wrapped the stump. I came back and asked if he had thought about getting a prosthesis. He simply shook his head.

The next day, during lunch, I was paged. It was Miss Dalton, Dr. Meyer's secretary.

"Dr. Meyer wants to see you in his office," she said over the telephone.

"When?"

"Right now. You better get over here."

The Chief had interviewed me for perhaps five minutes when I had applied for the residency before I went into the Navy. Since then, I had watched him operate every Saturday morning and had several times assisted him in surgery. He insisted on absolute quiet in the operating room. I doubted that he even knew the name of his residents. He was at least seventy years old, but looked twenty years younger. He was one of the best surgeons in the country.

Dr. Meyer was not only the Surgeon-in-chief, but he ran the entire hospital with an iron hand. He was a consummate politician whose power came from his surgical skill. The politicians, businessmen, rich tycoons, as well as the common people, flocked to him for surgery. He was very rich and powerful. We residents lived in fear and trembling of his wrath, but he was fair.

Miss Dalton sat on a straight-backed chair at her desk in a tiny alcove. She gave me a severe look and motioned towards the door of the sanctum.

A surgical journal lay open on the desk in front of Dr. Meyer. He didn't say hello or ask me to take a chair. His office was austere. The walls were painted the same bilious green as the rest of the hospital. The windows at his back overlooked Harrison Street. I stood at attention, feeling a little dizzy.

"You tried to shake down a patient," he said.

I was dumbfounded and didn't understand.

"No sir. I don't know what you are talking about."

"Giovani, the patient with the burned hand; he complained you tried to collect money."

His voice was soft, but his steely blue eyes seemed to bore into my very core. I remembered how surprised I was after seeing the well-dressed Mr. Giovani. It had never occurred to me that he might interpret my joke as an attempted shakedown.

During the Depression, when they were given only board and room, some interns tried to collect for treating patients. The usual technique was to say that if the patient paid he could get the "head doctor" to do his operation.

I was really upset. This was the first time anyone had questioned my honesty. It really hurt, because I respected the Chief.

"No, sir. Ask my intern. He heard the whole thing. If you really think this is true, I better quit the residency," I said.

I wasn't sure, but there appeared to be the trace of a faint smile on his lips.

"Don't let it happen again," he said.

I became more and more upset as I walked back to the operating room for the afternoon case. Miss "G" was hovering around while we scrubbed, and I told the interns about my session with Dr. Meyer. I was really angry by then.

She took me aside and whispered her advice just before the case began. I was already scrubbed and gowned.

"Doctor, don't have anything to do with Giovani," she said. "He is a gunman for the mob. The stove...they held his hand over a gas stove when he didn't pay a gambling debt."

A HAPPY ENDING

When the call came about an emergency chest consult in pediatrics, I was looking down the windpipe of a gentleman who had smoked a couple of packs a day for thirty years. The cancer was in his right main bronchus. I took a biopsy and called Rowley, the ped's resident as soon as I was finished. He sounded excited and a little worried.

"Hey, Tom, I got a kid with pus in his chest, mebbe an empyema. Can you come to the ped's ER?"

"Sure. I got one more case, won't take long," I said.

It was late in the day, and I really had planned on attending happy hour at the Monkey Room, but the kid might need chest drainage if he had an empyema. It was a bitterly cold January day, so I went down the stairs to the rat-infested, stinking tunnel that carried steam pipes to the morgue and hospital buildings, rather than face a howling wind off of Lake Michigan.

The pediatric emergency room consisted of a large waiting room surrounded by little curtained cubicles in the basement of the Children's Hospital. Bare bulbs hung from the ceiling over the women and children waiting to see a doctor on hard backless wooden benches. Rowley, the pediatric resident, was an Irish playboy, but worked hard to take care of kids. He led me to one of the curtained cubicles.

Eric was curled on his side on a hard wooden examining table with his hands over his head. There were bubbly noises in his chest, and with each breath, his nostrils flared as he tortuously sucked air through thick mucous. I watched his chest and counted nearly a hundred breaths a minute.

His bones were sharply etched under dark skin. His eyes and cheeks were sunken. The chart said he was nine years old, but he looked more like five. Every few minutes he had a painful bout of coughing, and thick green pus dribbled from the corner of his mouth. His skin was dry and hot. There was no resistance when I rolled him onto his back. His lips were blue, and the tongue was dry and covered with scummy mucous.

The bubbly rales in his chest were so loud a stethoscope wasn't necessary. The heart was shifted far over on the left side of his chest, which was completely dull to percussion. An empyema was a possibility, but I was puzzled by the shift of the heart to the side of dullness. Ordinarily, when fluid and pus builds up in the chest, the heart is shifted away, to the side of the good lung.

Eric's chest X-ray was taped to the view box. It was a typical fuzzy picture. Some old-time attendings commented that County X-rays were taken in rain and developed in fog. The left lung was completely opaque and the boy's heart was shifted all the way to the left chest wall. The right lung seemed to be clear. The X-ray confirmed that the boy had a major problem in the left lung, which was completely collapsed. There could be pus in the pleural cavity, but that seemed unlikely.

We went back to the tiny curtained alcove to talk with the elderly lady who had brought the boy to the hospital. The room was just large enough for an examining table, a chair, and a stool next to a miniscule desk for the intern to write a history. The lady, the boy's aunt, sat on the rusted metal chair with her hands folded over a black bible. She was slender, dressed in an old gray coat and black housedress. Her dark face was smooth, with high cheekbones and full, almost purple lips. Her short, crinkly gray hair fit over her head like a skullcap.

"Can you please tell us what you know about Eric?" I asked.

She stared at her thin bony hands and the bible for a long time.

"His momma was a addick."

She stopped speaking for a moment as if the fact that the boy's mother had been a drug addict explained everything.

"He was borned in Alabama, then she died with the TB, and the doctors say he had it too, in the lung and on the brain. They kep him in a TB hospital until a couple years ago, then I gotta call to come git him. They could'n find no other kinfolk. He's feeble in the head an always had weak lungs. I say, he was born sickly, and ain't never been right. He don do nothing but lay around and won't hardly eat an he never learnt to talk. He was comin on some better, until last week, when he got another fever an his cough got worse."

She paused for a moment and reached to stroke the boy's hot dry face.

"My docta just said ain't nothing he could do and to take him on out to the County, an so I brung him here."

The boy had not moved, but his eyes watched her face while she spoke. We asked her many questions about Eric, but she only shook her head. She couldn't remember the name of the hospital but was certain that he had been treated for tuberculosis.

Ward 46 was pretty much like the other floors in the Children's Hospital. A long corridor ran the length of the building. The nurse's station with cluttered desks for the ward clerk and interns was just off the elevators. Next door was the treatment room. This was where the interns sutured wounds, set fractures and changed bandages on burned children. It was almost always littered with dirty bandages, broken syringes, and bits of cast-off suture material. The screams of sick children echoed off its walls.

South of the nurse's station was a large room for sicker children and for those recovering from anesthesia. Down this corridor were more rooms with beds for girls. The north wing was for boys. There were often more than a hundred children ages one to twelve years on Ward 46. During winter, it overflowed with burned children, and in the summer, there were countless victims of auto accidents and kids who had fallen out of tenement windows. There was no way to isolate the many patients with infected dirty wounds from those with clean incisions.

We put Eric on the treatment table and let his aunt stay while we set up the oxygen tent and started intravenous fluids. Eric didn't cry when the nurse gave him a big shot of penicillin. It was nearly one o'clock in the morning when we had done everything possible to ease his breathing. It helped to put a long rubber tube down his throat to suck out the pus and mucous. He slept a little between coughing spells, but I didn't expect him to live through the night.

Sally Bliss, the charge nurse, was one of those rare, wonderful women who worked at the County because she really loved children. She and a handful of nurse's aides met the basic needs of the children with love and tenderness. Sally was a strong Iowa farmgirl who had come to County as a student nurse for more pediatric experience. She returned to County when she finished her nurse's training. Within a year she became the charge nurse on the children's surgical floor. She lived in the nurse's dormitory and worked ten to twelve hours a day. She had to do the work out of love, because nurse's pay at County was less than at any other hospital in the city.

Sally had come to the ward early, and by the time I arrived, she had made his bed, given him a cool bath and changed the oxygen tank. Some nurses at County became overwhelmed with the number of sick patients, but not Sally. She was always busy passing medications, giving orders to the nurse's aides, adjusting casts on kids with broken bones, and helping the interns with any of a thousand chores from changing dressings to suturing wounds. It was not unusual to see her charging down the corridor on the way to the treatment room with a child tucked under each arm. She was continuously cheerful and soothed each child's fears with lullabies and laughter. She really belonged on an Iowa farm with her own kids, but the ward was her second home.

"Hey, Dr. Tom, what's wrong with this little guy?"

"Sally," I answered, "your guess is as good as mine. His lungs are filled with pus and his mom had TB."

"Should we keep him in isolation?"

"Sure, and get some sputum for smear and cultures."

Eric clung to life, but made little improvement. His lung was still filled with mucous. He lay motionless and paid no attention to his surroundings. Attempts to give him a drink of water brought on spasms of coughing. He wouldn't eat. His only liquid and nutrition was from the intravenous fluids.

In the rare moments when Sally wasn't busy with another patient, she was at his bedside straightening his legs, or turning him into a more comfortable position. He finally became so weak, that the only way he was able to get rid of the mucous was when we suctioned his throat with a catheter.

On the morning of his third day in the hospital, I was on my way to the operating room, when Sally caught me at the elevator. She waved a lab report under my nose.

"Dr. Tom, look at this report. Eric has a staphylococcus in his sputum resistant to penicillin. He needs chloro and erythro."

I studied the lab slip, surprised to see that the lab had not found tuberculosis organisms.

"Sally, I don't know if we can get chloromycetin and erythromycin."

"You better try," she retorted.

We were just beginning to see bacteria that were resistant to the usual antibiotics. Several children had staphylococcal infections that literally thumbed their noses at penicillin. Chloromycetin and erythromycin, new antibiotics, were the only effective drugs for these terrible infections.

Unfortunately, they were very expensive and had not been approved for regular use in the County Hospital. I knew that there wasn't any use in arguing with Sally, so when my case was finished in the operating room, I went down to the assistant warden's office.

I tapped on her door.

"Come in, the door's open."

Helen Baker was a fine pediatrician and, unusual in the County, an administrator who cared for patients. She was, however, brusque and didn't tolerate nonsense, especially from a surgical resident.

"This is a tough case. He doesn't respond to penicillin and the lab report says he has a staphylococcus sensitive to chloromycetin and erythromycin."

She leafed through the chart and paid attention to the record of vital signs that showed a temperature curve, which spiked up and down.

"He still has a spiking fever."

She then held the X-ray up to the window.

"Hmm, looks like pneumonia, collapsed lung, bad."

She sat down and looked out her window onto Wood Street.

"Money is tight. The front office rations the new antibiotics, but this kid needs them."

She signed the requisition without more questions.

"Good luck, and let me know what happens."

Sally crushed the erythromycin tablets with sugar and water and forced the medicine down Eric's mouth. The chloromycetin had to be given by painful intramuscular injections.

After two days, Eric's fever came down and the left lung sounded better. Within a couple of days he took sips of juice from the nurse's aides and finally began to look around his room. It wasn't long before Sally had him propped up on pillows. He began to eat and drink.

In the meantime, we had a couple of better, clearer X-rays, which showed a small, scarred left lung containing cavities. The X-ray looked like a case of tuberculosis, but his sputum studies did not show any sign of tuberculosis germs. Finally, after Eric had been on the ward for about ten days, I gathered up my courage and showed his X-rays to Richard Holm, a thoracic surgeon.

Dr. Holm had worked at the TB sanitarium and knew as much about tuberculosis and chest surgery as anyone in the city. He was a tall, distinguished man, who walked with a limp as a result of a war wound. He was tough on us residents and called us "shoemakers" when we couldn't answer questions. He was a bit of a maverick with unorthodox ideas on the surgical treatment of tuberculosis, but he was an honest, no-nonsense doctor who was always interested in patients. We residents were a little afraid of him, but we respected his surgical skills.

He studied the X-rays intently for several minutes.

"What do you see?"

"Well, there's pneumonia in the left lung and the right lung is overexpanded."

"Is that all?" he asked.

I was embarrassed, and shifted my weight from one foot to another and avoided his piercing look. "Well, it looks like there are cavities."

He scowled and pointed to the X-ray.

"The upper spine is curved to the left. Next, notice the ribs. It looks like the kid has rickets. The trachea and heart are shifted to the left. This means that the left lung is smaller than normal. Also, notice the old scars and healed cavities. The pleura is thick on the left side, and his right lung has expanded to shift across the mediastinum."

I couldn't believe how much he saw in the X-ray and how much I had missed. Dr. Holm smiled at my discomfort.

"From the history, it sounds like he had tuberculosis which was cured, but the left lung was so damaged it is susceptible to new infections. There is pneumonia, but it is secondary to the underlying lung damage. The left lung isn't doing him any good and the infections will eventually kill him. Get him in shape. He needs a pneumonectomy."

Back on the ward, I told Sally what Dr. Holm had said about surgery.

"OK, I'll fatten him up," she said.

Eric got a little stronger every day. For a while, Sally and the aides spoonfed him, but then he was able to feed himself. Every afternoon, they gave him extra milk and cookies. We prescribed vitamins and iron and within a few days he was able to stand up and hobble about the ward. He was more alert but wouldn't talk and only made nonsense sounds as if he was mentally retarded. Sally thought he was trying to talk. He looked at comic books and pictures in magazines. One day on rounds with the interns, Sally stopped by his bed. Eric grabbed her hand and held on like he was drowning and she was a lifesaver.

"That kid isn't as dumb as we think," Sally said.

Within a week, his cough was better and his temperature was normal, but there were still rales and mucous in his left lung. He was stronger every day, but still not ready for major surgery. He began hanging out in the nurse's station during the day when Sally was on duty. Then he was animated and cheerful, but in the evenings he was morose and refused to get out of bed and wouldn't take his medicine.

When he was finally strong enough for an operation, his aunt came to the hospital. She sat by his bed, bible in lap, wearing the same housedress she had on when he first came to the hospital. I explained to her all about his lung and the X-ray and why he had to have surgery.

"Does he have to have an operachun, docta?" she asked.

"Yes, or he will have more bad spells," I said.

She took my pen and wrote her name on the bottom of the consent to surgery form. A tear rolled down her cheek and she patted Eric's face.

In the operating room, his eyes darted from our masked, unfamiliar faces to the instruments and then to the anesthesia machine. He was very quiet and held Sally's hand. It took us a while to get him ready because he had to have two intravenous lines for transfusions. The main risk while removing a lung was sudden blood loss from an injury to the pulmonary artery. Finally, the anesthetist put him to sleep with gas and ether.

It was a really dramatic moment. The first complete removal of a lung in an adult had been performed only twenty years before and no one could remember when a lung had been removed from a child in our hospital.

Dr. Holm stayed in the office chatting with Miss "G" and drinking coffee, while the intern and I rolled Eric on his side and carefully painted his skin from neck to belly button with iodine. We scrubbed together at the big sink across the hall, and then put on the gowns and gloves. Dr. Holm and I applied the sterile towels and sheets while the intern watched.

When everything was set, he made a swift curving incision from Eric's breastbone and around his chest. I clamped the bleeders with hemostats. When the bleeding was stopped, he cut deeper between the ribs, down to the adhesions that obliterated the pleural cavity. A normal lung is smooth and soft, but Eric's lung was hard and nodular and surrounded by dense adhesions.

It was a difficult dissection, but Dr. Holm made it look like a routine case. He put in a small chest retractor and cranked it open until the ribs were widely separated and he could get around the lung. We went after the bronchus first, so pus couldn't spill over into the good lung.

When the main bronchus was clamped and sutured, he dissected the pulmonary artery and the veins that were socked in with dense adhesions. He ligated them with silk ties, then cut the vessels between the ties and lifted the diseased lung out of the chest.

When Dr. Holm stepped away from the operating table leaving us residents to close the chest, Eric's blood pressure and pulse were perfectly stable. The whole operation lasted only about three hours. The lung that we removed was nothing much but scar and cavities. Treatment with streptomycin and isoniazid had cured the original tuberculosis, but left behind a destroyed lung.

I knew there was something about streptomycin that I should remember. It was the first antibiotic to prove effective against tuberculosis, but it had some undesirable side effects.

We wheeled Eric back to Ward 46, where Sally had a freshly made-up cot and an oxygen tent waiting in a side room. At first he had a lot of pain, but then he recovered quickly. After a few days, he could breathe easily without oxygen and his cough was miraculously gone.

Eric had the run of the ward but he usually hung around Sally. He ate everything in sight and was soon moved into a room at the far end of the hall with other boys. At first he was shy, but soon he was playing games and looking at picture books just like a normal boy. He spent hours watching the old black and white television set.

There were many other sick patients, and I didn't pay much attention to Eric after he had recovered from his operation. I assumed he was mentally retarded and would have simply sent him home to his aunt.

Sally seemed to have a special relationship with Eric. He clung to her while she was doing office work and followed her around the ward. She was a warm, motherly girl who came from a big family. Sally lived in the nurse's dormitory and didn't go out. Eric may have filled a void in her life. She stopped me in the hall one day with a copy of the Physician's Desk Reference.

"According to this, one of the side effects of streptomycin is deafness. I don't think he's retarded, just deaf."

It suddenly dawned on me that she could be right. Deafness was a side effect of streptomycin, which I should have remembered.

We went to Eric's room where the boys were watching a soap opera on TV. I put the earpieces of my stethoscope into Eric's ears and held the other end on the television. His face broke out into a big, beautiful smile and his eyes became round with delight. From then on, he watched television and listened to the sound with a stethoscope for hours on end. Soon he was repeating words and sentences that he had heard for the first time in his life.

He was making such wonderful progress that we did not have the heart to send him home. Sally talked to our social worker. Martha Edwards was one of those rare people who added a great measure of humanity to the County Children's Hospital. She was a plump, cheerful black woman with an office in a little cubbyhole on the first floor.

Her main job was to find homes for babies who had been abandoned and left at the hospital by their mothers. She brought warmth and enthusiasm to what must have been a heartbreaking job. We residents would often send poor parents to her office for carfare so they could get home. A long time later, I found out that the County had no budget for this, and that she had given money to people out of her own pocket.

Miss Edwards arranged for Eric to be seen at the Illinois Eye and Ear infirmary where he was fitted for a hearing aid. He soon became outgoing, cheerful, and quickly learned to talk. The public school system had teachers who taught classes for children hospitalized for long periods of time. Eric learned to read and almost caught up with children his own age. Even his usually dour aunt took an interest in his progress, so we finally let him go home in early June.

He returned for regular postoperative visits and often visited the ward with his aunt. He grew in height and weight and soon was a strong active boy. His aunt said that he was doing well in school and that some men in her church had taken an interest in him. Later, he attended a special school for deaf children.

Many years later, when I was a surgeon at the Children's Memorial Hospital, my secretary said that I had an appointment to see an old patient from the County. It was Eric. He was now a handsome, young man who had just graduated from high school and had a scholarship for college. I had always been worried about the capacity of his remaining right lung but my fears were put to rest. He was strong and muscular with only the scar to show for his pneumonectomy. His lung capacity was perfectly OK, and he was a champion golden gloves boxer!

Sally went back to Iowa, but remained a pediatric nurse. Eric was one of her many "children." She would be proud.

ABOUT THE AUTHOR

Dr. John Raffensperger received his M.D. from the University of Illinois and completed his surgical internship, residency and fellowship in Cardiac Surgery at Cook County Hospital. He also served in the United States Navy as Ship's Medical Officer. He has served as Director of Pediatric Surgery at Cook County Hospital and Director of Pediatric Surgery, and Surgeon-in-chief at Children's Memorial Hospital in Chicago until 1997. He is currently a Consultant in Surgery at Cook County Hospital and Children's Memorial Hospital, and is Professor of Surgery, Emeritus from Northwestern Medical School.

He has published numerous medical manuscripts and contributed to surgical textbooks and history. In addition, he has published several articles, both professional and of public interest. Dr. Raffensperger penned the quintessential history of Cook County Hospital, *The Old Lady on Harrison Street*. He continues to write, loves sailing, and lives with his wife, six stray cats and a Brittany named Rosie in the Lincoln Park area of Chicago.